THE ORGANIST AND
THE MAGISTRATE

ALSO BY THE AUTHOR

Sailor All at Sea

Bleak Encounter at the Cape

Parsonage and Parson: Coping with the Clergy

THE ORGANIST AND THE MAGISTRATE

Two tales of misadventure and crime, drawn from the personal knowledge and experience of the author in both of the title roles.

RICHARD TRAHAIR

The Book Guild Ltd

First published in Great Britain in 2023 by
The Book Guild Ltd
Unit E2 Airfield Business Park,
Harrison Road, Market Harborough,
Leicestershire. LE16 7UL
Tel: 0116 2792299
www.bookguild.co.uk
Email: info@bookguild.co.uk
Twitter: @bookguild

Typeset in 11pt Minion Pro

Printed and bound in the UK by TJ Books LTD, Padstow, Cornwall

ISBN 978 1915853 622

British Library Cataloguing in Publication Data.
A catalogue record for this book is available from the British Library.

This book is dedicated firstly to my two brothers, Stephen and Jonathan, with whose enthusiasm and joint enterprise I developed a keen interest in the pipe organ from an early age; and secondly to the memory of my father David and grandfather Edwin, each of whom long preceded me as a Justice of the Peace.

THE ORGANIST

A short story of espionage, murder and international conspiracy centred on the role of a pipe organ, in illustration of the workings of this, the King of Instruments.

INTRODUCTION

For several seconds very few in the audience realised that anything was wrong.

Hidden as he was behind the little Choir organ case, the organist could not be seen by his listeners as he played his recital before a packed abbey church.

In any case, he was approaching the final bars of Schoenberg's Variations on a Recitative in D with full diapason chorus, and his right elbow striking five adjoining keys simultaneously produced an effect barely more dissonant than the music printed on the page in front of him – not that he was seeing the score at that point, as his eyes had already glazed over.

It was not until his head drooped onto the Choir manual having played one chord with all Trumpet stops drawn that even the most unmusical person down in the pews below the organ gallery began to frown and look around at his neighbours for enlightenment.

As the appalling sustained blast of penetrating sound continued, the bossy little verger, who had been fussing around the church for most of the evening herding the ticket holders to their correct seats, took it upon himself to waddle importantly up the nave aisle and climb the stairs to the gallery.

After a long and pregnant pause, by which time most of the audience had stood up murmuring anxiously to one another, the verger's sheet-white face appeared over the balcony. At the same time the organ noise began to slide and subside in a banshee wail to diminuendo; a whimper and silence following his merciful decision to turn off the electric organ blower.

All eyes were now on the verger's terrified little face, as he struggled to find his voice and issue an articulate announcement.

After swallowing painfully a few times and making a couple of false starts he managed to address the sea of heads below him, who had by now fallen into speechlessness as they gazed up at him.

"L… ladies and g… gentlemen," he began. "I regret to have to inform you that… that… I regret… that is to say… *help!* He's been shot in the back of his neck."

CHAPTER ONE

Inspector Neish looked across his desk at his forensic colleague seated opposite him. He frowned.

"But surely," he muttered, "the angle of fire is all wrong. And we don't yet know whether it was a bullet or some other missile. The hospital has nothing for us so far, as he is still in theatre. Four hours on the operating table already, poor devil."

"Well," replied his colleague, "whatever it is may still be lodged in his skull. There is no sign of anything on the organ – apart from a small drop of blood on the bench and a smear on one of the keyboards, presumably where he fell forward. As for the angle, he may have turned his head to the left just as his assailant fired – maybe to pull out a stop-knob or two, or turn them or push them or whatever they do.

"Y'know, I was amazed when I was poking around up there this morning. I play the piano a bit, but that gizmo is something else. Three keyboards plus one you play with your feet, for goodness' sake, and these banks of control

1

panels with dozens of white knobs with odd names on them, plus a CCTV screen and some sort of calculator screen too with little green numbers lit up on it. Weird."

"CCTV?" interrupted the inspector. "If there's a screen then is there a camera?"

"No joy there. The camera is down below, covering the vicar and the choir. The organist can see them, but they can't see him – or her. Yes, I gather that their regular organist is a girl. This chap was just a guest recitalist – quite famous, I believe."

The inspector rattled his Biro against his teeth as a thought struck him.

"A girl, eh?" he mused. "And where was she last night, the host organist? I'd like a word with her, I think."

"Best of luck, then," replied the forensic officer. "Not my brief, of course, but the verger caretaker chappie who took me up there this morning happened to mention that she's gone AWOL. She didn't turn up for the recital, and she's not answering her phone. Not at home either, apparently."

*

It was not until the following day that the exhausted hospital consultant surgeon telephoned the police station.

Neish picked up his phone. "Thanks for getting in touch, Mr Adams. So how is the patient? ...I see. Very sorry indeed to hear that... yes, I'm sure you and your colleagues did everything you could...

"And cause of death? ...gracious me. 'A small steel tube

piercing the skin, hollow and containing what seems to be a toxin'… I'm just writing this down…

"Please preserve the bit of steel very carefully. My officer will be around to pick it up immediately. It very much looks like it, yes: a case of murder."

Neish laid his phone on the desk and contemplated the bare office wall opposite, expelling a long breath.

He jumped up from his chair. "Right," he said to himself, "here we go then."

Within minutes he had gathered his team in one of the cramped conference rooms. A detective constable was on his way to the hospital. The officer on duty in the church organ gallery was alerted to ensure that no one under any circumstances was permitted up the stairs.

"First things first," he began. "I want a list of all those in the audience last night, and any church officials there as well. Names and addresses with contact details where possible.

"Are any of you musical? And don't worry, I'm not about to ask you to shift a piano. I need a bit of insight into the playing of that box of tricks up in the church gallery.

"There's something odd about this incident. There was no one up in the gallery, as far as I can see, to jab or chuck the poison steel dart into the AP's neck. Only one staircase, in full view of the audience, and the verger confirms that no one was up there when he dashed up to see what was wrong."

A pause. Then a hesitant hand went up at the back of the conference room.

"Well, sir," came the quiet voice of a middle-aged detective constable, "as it happens I play the organ myself

9

in our Methodist chapel and understand the workings a bit, as I rebuilt a little old pipe organ with my brothers yonks ago when we were teenagers."

"Right, Jonathan," was the brisk reply from Inspector Neish, "come with me. We will poke around. Maybe there is a hiding place up there somewhere."

CHAPTER TWO

The vicar paced to and fro over his study carpet, the telephone to his ear, talking earnestly to his choirmaster.

"I can't understand it. Gillian is such a reliable person. Not turning up for choir practice is unheard of. Well, you play on Sunday and get one of the tenors to beat time. We'll manage.

"In the meantime, I'm going to go round to her flat and see if she's there. I gather she wasn't answering the door yesterday when Nick went round. She may be unwell."

Canon Haskins hung up and walked quickly across the churchyard to the old gatehouse, where the organist had a flat on the first floor, above the archway.

On a sudden thought, he had pocketed the spare keys to the flat which were kept in the vicarage safe.

At the top of the stairs, he knocked several times on the door. No answer.

"Gillian, are you there? It's Ben here. Give me a shout if you can hear me."

Nothing.

Ben Haskins frowned and made up his mind. Letting himself in through the door he stopped in the hall and called again, more quietly.

"Gillian, can I come in?"

Silence. Well, almost silence. All he could hear was a repeated bleep coming from some device in the kitchen. He peered cautiously around the open doorway.

The washing machine. Full of clothes and indicating a long-completed cycle. For how long? he wondered.

He then knocked tentatively on the closed bedroom door, and slowly opened it, rather dreading what he might discover.

The bed unmade; underclothes and jerseys strewn all over the floor; two open drawers; and an abandoned sports bag stuffed to overflowing with more clothes, clearly gathered in a hurry.

But of Gillian, not a sign or whisper.

Ben rapidly completed his investigation of the flat, which was otherwise revealing nothing remarkable, and returned the way he had come, locking the door behind him.

On his return to the vicarage, the vicar heard the telephone ringing again. The choirmaster once more.

"Ben, I've just had a call from the police station. I'm afraid we can't use the organ tomorrow, or for the foreseeable future, as they need to carry out more forensic examination up there in the gallery.

"I asked about the poor recitalist on Thursday evening. He must have suffered a severe injury of some sort – or maybe it was a heart attack. You know Nick as well as I do: a good verger but a bit highly strung. He yelled out something about Sir John being shot in the back of the head, but surely not.

"Anyway, the police are refusing to say anything. All very odd."

Canon Haskins sat back in his chair and thought long and hard. His pastoral ministry in this large town was wide and varied, and he was no stranger to personal crisis amongst his parishioners. He was all too accustomed to being called out to support and comfort those in distress or emergency, and frequently took upon himself the practical or administrative tasks which such incidents generated for people in no state to deal with them themselves.

But suddenly, out of the blue, two complete mysteries now, right on his own doorstep. A visiting organist severely injured, or worse (gosh, yes, he must put something in the church accident book); and his own organist, who had totally vanished without leaving a note or message of any kind.

A bit of a coincidence, both being organists. What on earth did a wooden case full of about four thousand tubes of lead, wood and tin have to do with it?

No. This had to be about the two people themselves. What did he know about either of them?

Sir John Winnersley FRCO was, of course, well known, or had been in his prime. He was now pushing eighty, but two decades ago he was a renowned concert recitalist. He had retired to this town, and in fact lived within walking distance of the church. Beyond that, the vicar knew nothing much about him at all. A widower, still reasonably active socially and looked after by an unmarried daughter.

And what about his church organist, Gillian? She had been in post for three years, arriving with excellent references from her last two positions, as organist of a city church in Durham and then at the King's Chapel in Gibraltar, which was attached to the official residence of the Governor there. She was single and in her mid-thirties, a quiet and rather solitary figure who seemed to prefer her own company to the social life of the parish.

Canon Haskins recalled that Gillian had spoken warmly of her time in Gibraltar.

The chapel organ had been nothing much to speak of, but her role with the King's Chapel Singers and the concerts laid on by family members of the three British armed forces based in Gibraltar had been great fun. Life there had been good, but the Canon had the impression that Gillian had left and returned to England in something of a hurry.

He had no information on her wider family. She never stayed away from home as far as he was aware.

Until now.

CHAPTER THREE

Inspector Neish and Detective Constable Mayne took a close look at the tiny steel item enclosed in a sealed transparent bag, recovered from the hospital by the forensics officer. It was a short thin needle, apparently detached or broken off from a standard disposable medical syringe. At its blunt end it had been thickened slightly with two rounds of insulating tape, while its sharp end still showed, under a magnifying glass, a smear of blood diluted with a drop of amber liquid.

More of the liquid from the hollow needle had been sent for analysis at Porton Down in Wiltshire, as the local forensic laboratory had been unable to identify it.

"Right, Constable," Neish concluded, straightening up from his examination of the murder weapon, "let's go on up to the church and you can explain to me what the recitalist would have been doing when this bit of needle stabbed him in the neck. At the moment I am completely baffled."

Jonathan Mayne led the way up the gallery stairs, and the officer on duty stood aside.

"Give us a tune, then, Jonathan," Neish said. "I've never watched an organist at work."

The constable slid onto the bench and familiarised himself with the layout of the stop-knobs and the switches for lights and blower at the console.

Pressing the blower button, he drew a Lieblich Gedecht and a four-foot flute on the Swell, and a Stopped Diapason on the Great with a soft sixteen-foot on the Pedal.

"What's that swishing noise, then?" enquired the inspector.

"That's the blower forcing the wind into the reservoir

down at the back," replied his constable. "Then when I play a note, like this, a 'pallet' or valve releases wind into the foot of the pipe and the pipe then 'speaks', just like playing a penny whistle with your mouth."

He played a short few bars of Handel. Neish watched from the treble end of the console. There was no room at all to squeeze behind the player, as the bench was only six inches away from the back of the Choir organ case that hid the organist from view down in the church pews.

Neish scratched his head. How on earth did that little needle pierce the back of Sir John's neck right in the middle, at the top of his spinal cord? Even if he had turned his head to the left at that very moment, a needle shot from the right would still not have entered centrally. And there had been no one standing or squatting to his right or to his left; nobody on the gallery or the gallery stairs at all. Where the heck had it come from?

The inspector's musings returned to the music. "Come on, Mr Organist, this is sounding a bit dull. Give it some oomph. I thought organs were supposed to blast out louder than a brass band, and shake the building."

Jonathan Mayne surveyed the upper regions of the stop jambs. He pressed piston six on the Great, and drew the Tromba and four-foot Cornet on the Choir with Great to Pedal and a full Swell chorus with the swell box open.

"Are you quite sure, sir?" he asked with a smile. "This will lift the lid off."

"Go for it, chum," came the reply.

With that, the opening bars of 'Land of Hope and Glory' ricocheted off the noble stone walls of the grand old mediaeval church, a cacophony of sound that almost made the inspector lose his balance. The other officer at the far end of the gallery looked decidedly alarmed.

And then Constable Mayne flicked out the thirty-two-foot Open Diapason and sixteen-foot Ophicleide on the Pedal division and trod his left foot firmly onto the bottom G of the pedal board. The thunderous effect was thrilling, but the climax then followed with a three-note major chord high up on the Choir manual for the full Trumpet chorus.

The same Trumpet chorus played by Sir John Winnersley two days previously, seconds before he slumped forward and lost consciousness.

*

The magnificent final chord rolled around the building and drained away into its nooks and crannies.

Detective Constable Mayne thumbed the General Cancel piston and looked up with a slight frown.

"Oh dear," he said, "that's a pity."

"What's that, Jonathan? Can't hear a word. You've completely deafened me."

"Well, sir, one of the Tromba pipes is not speaking. There was a distinct gap in that last chord."

"No, can't say I noticed. I was concentrating on not bursting an ear drum."

Jonathan Mayne swivelled around on the organ bench to face the back of the Choir organ case. This had two large hinged doors for access to its innards for maintenance and tuning the pipes.

"It may be a simple problem of the pipe foot not sitting properly on the soundboard."

He swung open both doors and peered inside.

A long pause.

"Hello, what the hell's that?" came his voice from the cavernous interior.

"Boss, come around onto the bench and take a look at this."

Neish and Mayne sat alongside each other and studied the intricate contents of the case.

Ranks and ranks of pipes of all shapes and sizes, metal as well as wooden, filled the space in graceful parabolas, all firmly secured with their feet held by rackboards.

All except one pipe, from the Tromba rank, which was absent, leaving the parabola looking like a smile with a tooth missing.

Mayne found the light switch for the case interior. Now they could see the components quite clearly.

Where the foot of the missing pipe would have been lodged in its windway hole in the top of the soundboard, a large cork had been jammed. Protruding through the cork was a narrow copper tube which wound its way upwards and in between the adjacent serried pipe ranks to the rear of the case, where its end was fastened horizontally to a rackboard pillar with insulating tape.

On close inspection the police officers could now just make out a small hole drilled in the panel of the door which, when shut, married up precisely with the open end of the copper tube.

The position of the tube and its hole in the door was

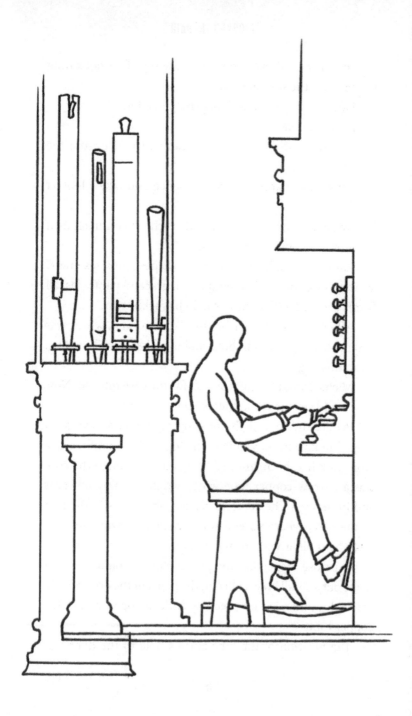

central to the organ bench and at a height that corresponded accurately to the exposed neck area of anyone sitting on it no more than about four inches away.

CHAPTER FOUR

Mayne was silent for a while, thinking hard. Then he nodded to himself and addressed his perplexed superior.

"Quite clever, sir," he muttered. "Someone knew exactly what he was doing; someone who understood all about organs.

"This rank of Tromba pipes is on what organ-builders call high pressure. To you and me it is not high at all, compared with, say, a kettle boiling or a car tyre pump. This will be on what we call about fifteen inches of wind. Blowing through the open foot of its pipe, it couldn't possibly propel any object, even a light dart.

"However, compressed through this tiny narrow copper tube, the wind will have come up against the thickened end of the needle lightly jammed into the end of the tube when the organist played that particular note. If the note is held for long enough the pressure in the tube will have built up sufficiently to unplug the obstruction and shoot the needle that short distance, four or five inches, into the back of the player's neck."

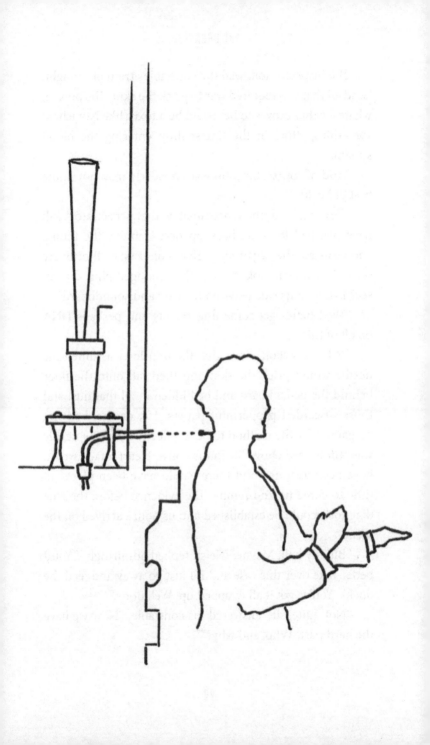

The inspector followed the constable's train of thought. "And all that was required was to prick the skin. The poison, whatever that proves to be, could be a toxin like Novichok, something lethal in the tiniest drop entering the blood stream.

"And of course, Sir John was an elderly man not in the best of health."

"Yes, sir, and then presumably the perpetrator will have planned to come back up here, remove the tubing and reinstate the organ pipe. That would take all of thirty seconds. And sir, look, there is the dislodged pipe, do you see? Lying on its side between the case and soundboard."

"We'd better get some fingerprints and perhaps DNA on all of this."

"What I reckon, sir, is that the murderer assumed the needle would prick the skin and then fall onto the floor behind the pedal board and be hidden in all that dust and those discarded peppermint papers. He, or she, had not bargained for the method to be so effective that the needle was still lodged above Sir John's collar. Heart attack would have been assumed and there would have been plenty of time to come up and remove the evidence before the true diagnosis could be established and us police arrived on the scene."

"Bloody hell, Mayne," Neish replied admiringly. "You'd better take over this case and I'll just go away and feed the ducks. You've got it all wrapped up. Well done."

"Not quite, sir," answered his constable. "Now we have the hard part. Who, and why?"

*

As they were leaving the church by the south door, the police officers met the vicar bustling in.

"Ah, gentlemen," breathed Canon Haskins with much relief, "I am glad to see you. We have another mystery on our hands, I'm afraid. My organist, Gillian Dams, has disappeared, and apparently in a bit of a hurry."

He reported what he had discovered in her flat. "It is completely out of character. She failed to turn up on Thursday evening to greet the guest organist, poor Sir John; and didn't arrive for choir practice last night. She never goes away – and I have absolutely no idea where she may have gone now."

"Thank you, Vicar," answered Neish. "I think I share your concern. Leave this to us; we will take steps to find Miss Dams. Apart from anything else, we need to talk to her about the incident on Thursday evening.

"Miss Dams may well be able to help us with our enquiries into Sir John Winnersley's death."

The Canon stared at the inspector for several seconds. "Really? Good heavens, I don't see how she could assist you there, I'm sure."

"Matters of a technical nature, sir, concerning the organ," explained Constable Mayne.

"Oh, right," said the vicar doubtfully. "Well, if that is relevant I will leave it to you. Please let me know as soon as you find her, won't you?"

And he passed on into the church.

Saturday afternoon was verging on the early loss of light of a dull and drizzly October evening as the two officers emerged into the Close from the abbey church. A light wind was scattering the first fallen chestnut leaves over the cobbles.

Neish shivered in his lack of overcoat. "I'm beginning to think that our Miss Dams has some awkward questions to answer – when we find her. Who had a better opportunity than her to rig up that poison dart contraption, or had a better understanding of how it might be made to work as a murder weapon?

"And what's she got against poor old Winnersley? Seems to be taking professional musician's jealousy a bit far."

"Shall I put in for a search warrant, sir?" responded Mayne. "It's Sunday tomorrow but I can get the court legal adviser on the phone at home, and we may be given a local magistrate to hear the application in the morning. It's a good chance to make a thorough search of Miss Dams' flat. The vicar said he had the keys."

"Yep, you do that, Constable. I'm off home before I freeze to death. I'll put an officer on at the archway flat first. Report to me then at 1100 hours tomorrow. Goodnight."

The inspector turned his coat collar up and, hunching his shoulders, mooched off into the gathering gloom.

Jonathan Mayne retraced his steps towards his car and, passing the church porch, his eye caught a brightly coloured poster flapping gently in the damp breeze. He stopped to read it:

ORGAN RECITAL
Thursday 20th October, 7:30pm

RICHARD TRAHAIR

Thomas Canterer FRCM
Internationally renowned
Tickets from parish office
Or at the door

Across the printed name of the recitalist had been pasted a
narrow strip of paper, now coming adrift in the damp wind,
overprinted with the name 'Sir John Winnersley'.

CHAPTER FIVE

A magistrate in the town had agreed to hear the warrant application at her home on the Sunday afternoon, and had granted it not only in connection with a possible murder suspect or witness, but for the personal safety of Miss Dams as a missing person.

Constable Mayne collected the flat keys from the Canon and, on a dry, chilly Sunday evening, entered the gatehouse apartment with Inspector Neish.

The state of the rooms remained as described by the Canon on his visit two days earlier. The washing machine was still plaintively bleeping.

Mayne turned it off. "What are we looking for, boss?" he enquired.

"Something, anything, that might explain Gillian's sudden flight from home. Was she trying to escape justice or is there some other reason?

"From what you spotted on the notice board yesterday, Mayne, Winnersley does not seem to have been the intended victim of the poisoned dart. The change of recitalist was only made on Thursday morning, when Mr Thomas Canterer phoned the vicar to say that he had sprained an ankle and couldn't play after all. Sir John obligingly stepped in at only a few hours' notice."

"Poor old bloke," commiserated Mayne, "just doing a good turn and ending up dead, literally on his last chord."

After half an hour they could find nothing to point to where Gillian Dams had gone – no visa receipt for a train ticket or flight; no accommodation booking form or evidence of an ATM withdrawal. Her laptop charger cable lay on her desk, but the laptop was not there. Presumably she had taken it with her.

The old oak desk in front of the elegant eighteenth-century sash window of the sitting room was the only location of any paperwork in the premises, which made the search relatively straightforward. Between them, the police officers carefully perused the contents of each drawer: documents, letters and statements. All appeared to be perfectly innocuous and unsurprising.

From the very bottom left-hand drawer, Mayne extracted a large manila envelope on which had been scrawled in felt-tip pen 'King's Chapel Gib'. Inside was a motley collection of papers dating back four or five years previously. He recalled Canon Haskins mentioning Gillian's earlier employment. There were old concert programmes from the Chapel Singers; an assortment of photographs, presumably that she had taken, of the choir, the rock, the incongruously British street scenes, and the ships and boats in the colourful harbour. Noticeably absent were photos of any individual people – friends or colleagues, or even family. The group photos of the choir were the only images that recorded personal acquaintances at all.

There was also a small sheet of regulation-size miniature passport prints of Gillian herself (Mayne presumed). Face on, and with no attempt at sensitive lighting, she was still revealed as a startlingly attractive young woman. A classic heart-shaped face and chin, slightly retroussé nose, penetrating dark eyes and lashes, and glossy straight black hair swept back into a single loose plait wound into a coil at her nape on the left side. She was quite brown-skinned, from sunshine or genealogy. Welsh, perhaps? Or Celtic anyway.

Mayne found buried in the envelope some mixed correspondence. The King's Chapel was Church of England, whose diaspora had proudly exported much of the Church's administrative eccentricities, not least concerning its lay employees. Here were her contract of employment, endless certificates of safeguarding and enhanced DBS, the Diocese of Europe handbook, and an official letter from the Governor welcoming her to her post. His Excellency the Governor of Gibraltar appeared to have some central role in the matter, no doubt because the chapel was attached to his official residence.

As indeed was the flat allocated to the chapel's Director of Music. There were a few photographs of its interior – small but neat and adequate for a single person, and with plenty of daylight.

Then Mayne took out a smaller envelope, which had been partially re-sealed. He carefully peeled back the flap and withdrew a single sheet of paper.

This too was a letter from the Governor, on his magnificently decorated headed notepaper. But this one was entirely handwritten. Mayne noted the date, just a few weeks before Gillian Dams had started her new job here in the abbey church.

My dear Gillian,

Formal thank-yous have already been made to you for your valuable contribution to the life of the King's Chapel, notably your development of the Singers and the involvement of members of the armed forces and their spouses stationed here.

This letter is for your eyes only. You and I, and of course your 85 Albert principal, are the only people who know the reason for your prompt and urgent departure from Gibraltar last month.

I sincerely regret the circumstances in which this became necessary, for your own security and for the sake of the service for which you operate. I do wish that it could have been otherwise, as you were making good headway.

Keep your head down, my dear, and stay safe. You have music to uphold you.

With deepest respect,

A... M...

Constable Mayne fanned his face thoughtfully with the buff envelope for a moment or two.

"Have a read of this, boss. I have a feeling there is more to Miss Gillian Dams than so far has met the eye."

The inspector reached for the letter and read it rapidly.

"Hmm, clearly a creature of mystery. Whatever it means it might at least explain why she appears so secretive.

"What does His Excellency the Governor mean by 'the service for which you operate'? And 'your own security'? Surely he cannot be referring to the Church of England?"

"No, sir, I suspect something a lot closer to the Establishment than the established Church," Mayne ventured.

"Oh, very good, Mayne, nice one. Well, there's nothing more for us here, I think.

"Go and find out how the team is getting on with IDs for all the audience on Thursday. I'm beginning to suspect that is going to be a waste of time.

"This murder was self-inflicted when he played that final extended cord. The murderer herself – sorry, or himself – could have been miles away at that moment.

"I'm going to talk to the Super. We need to interpret the Governor's letter, especially what he meant by 'your principal'. That might explain things."

Suddenly the inspector's phone bleeped.

"Inspector Neish, Budgen from forensics here. I've just had a call from Porton Down. The Winnersley case. That broken needle contains something called VX toxin. One of the most instantly lethal there is. Almost impossible for any private individual to obtain. There would be a major organisation behind this, or even a state.

"Porton are refusing to return the needle; they're keeping it under top security.

"They are also sending two operatives to decontaminate the area around and behind the organist's bench. Some of that woodwork may need to be dismantled, removed and burnt."

Inspector Neish blinked and swallowed hard. For a second or two he stared out through the large sash window. The October sky had cleared for a watery setting sun to emerge and reflect off the wet chestnut and lime trees across the abbey Close, their leaves flashing in the gusty wind.

Out there was normality, a picturesque picture-postcard view totally alien to the images now crowding his mind.

"All right, thank you, Joe," he eventually replied, staring meaningfully at Constable Mayne to gain his close attention. "And I will immediately alert the mortuary and the undertaker to keep hands well clear from the deceased. Rubber gloves only, immediately and separately bagged and labelled. We won't identify the toxin to the undertaker. Cheers, Joe.

"Mayne," he continued without drawing breath, "it was something called VX, an instant killer. Get on to the mortuary and funeral director PDQ.

"Oh, and Porton are going to pull apart the organ woodwork. We need to photograph everything before they get there, all the mechanism and immediate vicinity, from every possible angle. Those photos will be crucial for CPS evidence in court. I realise it's Sunday, but just get that idle official snap-happy out of bed and along to the church with his lights and cameras – now."

CHAPTER SIX

Osmundson & Rushworthy were a small but respected firm of organ-builders, established in 1894 and for more than seventy-five years the designers and makers of small, modest instruments for churches and chapels throughout the West Country. In those days they laid their own lead and tin sheets and formed their own pipework as well as exquisite joinery for the wooden ranks and their pitch pine or oak organ cases and consoles.

After the retirement of the last Osmundson, the firm reluctantly decided to cease construction, and in recent decades had developed a specialist business in organ repairs, maintenance, re-voicing and tuning instruments of any builder as well as their own earlier examples.

But times were hard. Parish church congregations and the members of Baptist and Methodist chapels in the small towns and villages, whose organs were the firm's bread and butter, were increasingly struggling to raise each year the funds needed to pay 'parish share' for training, paying and housing their clergy, with little left over to maintain their buildings, many of which were of major historic importance.

Their organists were gradually falling away through old age or infirmity, and the younger generation seemed less interested in taking up the instrument. Consequently, a growing number of little pipe organs remained silent, and musical accompaniment of hymns increasingly relied upon MP3 recordings or, at best, a pianist with a digital keyboard.

What was the point in paying three hundred pounds to get the old organ routinely adjusted and tuned?

Osmundson & Rushworthy's business began its slow demise.

Then one day, at the turn of the year in which these momentous events at the abbey church took place, a young man called at Osmundson's premises offering to be taken on as an apprentice without salary. He seemed very keen, and came with two glowing references, one of which was on the headed notepaper of the British Institute of Organ Studies.

The firm was delighted, so pleased in fact that they did not trouble to contact the referees. Perhaps this would be a chance for the company to restore its fortunes, if necessary by diversification, through the next generation.

Young Henry was well-spoken and intelligent, and must have been quite well heeled as money never appeared to be a problem.

Osmundson's works were on the southern edge of Bristol, now in a nondescript steel warehouse building on a characterless industrial estate. Their original works further north into the city had long ago been sold and demolished for a shiny new block of long-leasehold apartments.

Henry was quick to learn the elements of the trade. His particular interest lay in electro-pneumatic key and slider action and the range of wind pressures appropriate for different ranks of stops – open-footed wooden pipes, soft tin flutes and the great flared reed pipes that 'spoke' through vibrating brass tongues. Organ wind pressure had a unique form of measurement determined by the height in inches of a tube of water of specified dimensions set into a piece of equipment that could be placed over any windway hole so that the lead weights sitting on the wind reservoir beneath could be adjusted until the correct pressure was reached. On large organs several separate wind chests were required for different pressures, and on more modern instruments there were now more sophisticated methods of achieving the desired number of 'inches'.

All of this became Henry's speciality, alongside the routine duties of cleaning and re-tuning. After about six months, the boss started to send Henry out on his own to simple and straightforward jobs on little single manuals. Henry owned a classic MGB convertible in racing green that was his pride and joy.

*

The grand Gray & Davison organ in the abbey church had, since its rebuild and restoration twelve years previously, been maintained by its restorers, Harrison & Harrison of

Durham, to the highest standards always associated with that famous firm.

One hot day in August of this year in question, an immaculate shiny green sports car had drawn up on the gravel parking area at the west of the church, in front of the dignified vicarage. A strong and gusty warm wind was furiously fluttering the St George flag high up on its tower flagpole. Green leaves of many shades were prematurely uncoupling from their branches and whisking diagonally off the limes and chestnuts to touch down briefly on the cobbles and take off again in coordinated spiral like a murmuration.

It had been a Tuesday. No one was about. The church was open but unmanned except for a small grey-haired helper in a blue apron, way up in the chancel cleaning the brass lamp stems along the choir stalls.

The young man who had arrived in the MGB entered the church and looked carefully around him. He studied the organ gallery briefly, glanced eastwards and spotted the cleaner busy at her task.

He strode confidently up the central nave aisle and, with a friendly smile and short wave, attracted her attention.

"Hello," he said, "sorry to interrupt. I just wanted to let you know that I have been sent from the organ-builders Harrison & Harrison to carry out a few adjustments and checks to the pipework that we had no time for at our last re-tuning visit. I won't make a noise, so just ignore me, OK?"

"Right you are, young man, thanks for letting me know," she replied, rubbing vigorously at a brass standard without looking up.

He returned to the foot of the gallery, and ignoring the chain across the lower stair that held a suspended card reading 'No Public Access', he ascended to the top and walked along the gallery to the central organ loft. Here he sat on the end of the organist's bench and studied the layout of the console and the casework above him.

From a pocket he withdrew a small camera, a Sony Cybershot G, and took several shots of the console and pedal board, with close-ups of the stop jambs focusing on the stop names inscribed on the face of their ivory knobs.

With a grunt of satisfaction he noted the names of the Choir organ ranks, and opened the access door at the back of the Choir case. Here he took several more close-up photographs and, taking a five-foot tape measure from another pocket, made a note on a piece of paper of a number of distances and measurements.

All this he did without haste, knowing he was completely secluded behind the Choir case from being seen by the cleaner or anyone else in the church below.

Pocketing his equipment, he retraced his steps to the nave, exchanged a wave with the lady in the apron and left the building.

He departed cautiously down the gravel drive in his car and, leaving the town, accelerated fast onto the dual carriageway.

He had not, however, headed for his place of employment in Bristol. Instead he had driven north-east to the M4, and had made for a certain destination in the West End of London.

CHAPTER SEVEN

Inspector Neish pressed 'end of call' and rubbed his ear. "Blimey," he said aloud, although there was no one else in the room. "Spare me from angry men of God."

He had just had a rather one-sided twenty-minute phone conversation with Canon Haskins, who clearly had his choirmaster in the background egging him on. Why was it necessary for two men in white space suits and helmets to take away in their blue flashing van the organist's bench, the entire back of the Choir organ case and much of its innards, having added insult to injury by first spraying a foul-smelling green chemical fluid all over the organ loft floor and the pedal board? Who was going to pay to replace them or put them back together when the police had got round to deciding how poor Sir John met his death?

Neish had murmured something about informing their insurance company in the first instance.

"I will, I will," growled the vicar. "Michael Angell at the Ecclesiastical Insurance Office will sort you all out, you wait and see."

The beleaguered inspector sighed and stomped off to Comms. The press would be onto this at any minute, he knew, and prepared statements were now necessary. At all costs the phrase 'VX toxin' must be kept under wraps.

The superintendent met him in the corridor.

"Come in here a minute, will you, Simon. The Winnersley plot is thickening."

Simon Neish followed his senior officer into an empty office.

"I've been onto Intelligence in Bristol. They told me to talk to the Met. Scotland Yard phoned me an hour ago and I explained both the poison ID and the Governor's letter to the Dams woman. '85 Albert' is an oblique reference to the headquarters of MI6 at Vauxhall Cross. Our vanished lady organist is beginning to look like Secret Service. If so, and if she is still on the level – and not our murderer – then MI6 – SIS – will know where she is.

"Unfortunately, they certainly wouldn't tell us country bumpkins. This is getting all way beyond my pay grade."

"But sir," replied Neish, "we need to speak to her urgently. The Winnersley fatality is our problem, not theirs."

*

Back in August, the green MGB had slid smoothly into a private covered car park off Berkeley Square in London. Its driver went up some concrete steps in one murky corner of the darkened space and pressed a button to one side of a heavy steel door. He spoke a short password into the intercom and the door opened by controlled hydraulics.

Once inside he strode along a corridor and let himself into a small office with his own key.

Sitting at a grey metal desk that supported a sophisticated array of digital equipment and a laptop, he plugged in his camera and downloaded the images and measurements he had taken at the abbey church. On a design program he sketched a 3D drawing of the mechanism he had formulated as he drove up to Town, attached it with the photos to a brief report and pressed 'send'.

Somewhere further along the passage, or for all he knew in a different building or country altogether, his message was instantly translated into Catalan and Spanish, encrypted and dispatched to his unknown paymaster.

His role was almost complete. If his ingenious recommendation was approved, he would acquire the simple components and await instruction for the right moment to install them in the organ case.

The tiny phial of VX toxin would then be deposited in a safe box in the premises for him to collect, together with a pair of research-lab protective gloves.

It was not to be until October that he was instructed to proceed.

He returned to his car and set off back to Bristol and to his ostensible career with Osmundson & Rushworthy.

*

And now, October had arrived, and with it the momentous events at the abbey church.

Jonathan Mayne returned to the organist's flat over the

gatehouse to see what else he might find, in light of what he and his inspector had learned of Gillian Dams' apparent occupation as some kind of spy. Her role as abbey organist might merely be a cover.

Sifting through a pile of magazines and old newspapers on the coffee table, Mayne noticed a two-week-old copy of the local *Western Daily Gazette* that had been carefully folded back with an inner page exposed. A bold headline read 'Spanish claim to Gibraltar from Brexit', and underneath a short interview with the hapless Conservative MP for the west of the county attempting to minimise the risk mooted in the article's headline.

Mayne picked up the paper and skimmed through it. An editorial article drew attention to the evidence reported by a county councillor with a family Catalan connexion that subversive attempts could be expected in certain Spanish quarters to undermine British authority in Gibraltar, as part of a political campaign to reopen the issue of sovereignty following the departure of the UK from the European Union.

Of course, Mayne acknowledged to himself it was only natural that Gillian would have been interested in that piece in view of her own recent job there in the King's Chapel.

Another brief entry in the same paper caught his eye: 'ORGAN RECITAL: the St Aldhelm Abbey church organist Miss Gillian Dams will be giving a performance of nineteenth-century music in the Abbey on Thursday the 20th October in the evening. Further details in due course'.

Mayne was about to pass over this and continue his browse through the pile of magazines, when he paused and frowned.

Thursday the 20th October? But surely that was the evening of the demise of Sir John Winnersley? He had taken the place of Thomas Canterer at the last minute. Hang on, thought Jonathan Mayne, this is beginning to get complicated.

Then suddenly, a piece of the jigsaw fell into place. Of course! Our mysterious SIS agent Gillian had been the intended *victim* of the attack, not the culprit. Whoever was behind the attempted assassination had based their plan on the announcement in the regional newspaper.

Mayne immediately phoned the vicar.

"Oh yes, that's right," confirmed Canon Haskins, "Gillian was originally intending to give the recital but had some urgent business in London and had to find someone else. Fortunately she knew Thomas Canterer from her time in Durham, and he was happy to come and play instead, until of course he had to pull out with a sprained ankle at the last minute.

"We didn't have time to re-advertise all these new arrangements, except for putting up a few new posters around the town.

"Anyway, when are we getting our organ back?"

CHAPTER EIGHT

In a narrow, dusty backstreet of Cadiz in southern Spain, up a flight of stairs in a small room shut off in deep gloom from the heat of the day, sat three men.

One of them, a swarthy fellow with narrow eyes set just too closely together to instil confidence, was speaking.

"Now, listen. I've got new instructions from Madrid. We are to create an incident over on the Rock, designed to shake up the complacency of the ordinary folk who live there. Our job is to make them jittery, to ask themselves how long they could hold on to British occupation of our land and defy the rights of our great nation to take back what belongs to us."

His two colleagues nodded in agreement, one of them swearing colourfully under his breath.

"So," continued the envoy from the capital, "this time we've got to get it right. Our last attempt at their Governor was discovered too soon by that wretched woman in the Governor's residence sticking her nose in just at the wrong moment.

"Anyway, she's gone back to the UK, and I'm told that our guys over there are on her tail, and good luck to them. She needs to be put away, for good. If she was a British agent and not just some choir mistress, it means they're onto us and we must work fast if we're to succeed this time.

"Here's the plan. Either of you ever seen that James Bond film *The Living Daylights*?"

"Oh, yeah," replied the brighter of his two listeners, "I remember that. A pistol hidden in the pew of the Gibraltar Governor's Chapel. But the scheme didn't work, did it? 007 foiled the plot."

"Look," snapped their boss, "there's no James Bond this time, and this is for real.

"That British Governor has taken to attending services in the chapel regular, so we can rely on him being there when we strike. Now you, Mario, look a bit more English than our friend here, 'specially if you have a proper shave for a change and get a haircut. One of these King's Chapel services is going to be official, and the people there will all be in their uniforms. There will be some from the navy, some army and a few air force. I've got hold of a genuine British Army get-up. 'Lance corporal' or something.

"You, Mario, are going to attend that event; go in at the last minute and stay right at the back. You're a good shot and it's not a very large hall. You can't miss."

"Oh, sure, boss. And then their entire armed services grab hold of me and I'm in clink for the rest of my life for murder.

"Or am I supposed to turn the gun on myself and be a martyr to the Kingdom?"

"No, you fool. You're not shooting to kill, just to fire close enough to give them all a shock. Our team's propaganda and the press will be lined up to maximise the political and international fallout.

"As for your carcass, Mario, that's where your friend here comes in.

"You, my friend, will join the cleaning firm used by the Governor's staff, two weeks before target day. That's all arranged. On the previous day, the Saturday, you'll place a large smoke bomb with a timer inside the organ case in the north-west corner of the chapel. That's the left-hand side looking up to the altar, at the back.

"At the rear of the organ is an opening panel, and inside is the wind reservoir, which has a flat top with a few bars of lead sitting on top, Lord knows what for. Anyway, you place the bomb on that, set the timer for the following morning – you will be given the required time – and close the panel.

"Your main job is to not be seen by any of your cleaner colleagues going in behind the organ or coming back out again. Got it?

"OK. Then, Mario, as soon as the smoke bomb goes off and everyone is distracted, you fire your automatic—"

"What automatic, boss?" Mario interrupted.

"Listen, you oaf, and I'll tell you. You'll be given a small automatic and you will stuff it down your trousers – for which it will have my deepest sympathies – and you then fire towards the Governor, but for God's sake aim high.

"Don't then rush to escape. Drop the gun quickly and point towards the organ screen and shout something like 'over there'. Even you can manage two words of English.

"Then in the general mêlée, you leave the building with everyone else, coughing and spluttering in the smoke.

"Once outside, you disappear. You're good at that."

*

The quietest of the Spaniards meeting in Cadiz, and destined to become a temporary member of the Governor's cleaning contractors, left the briefing session in deep thought. He realised that he had to establish quickly the date of this special chapel service. In the meantime he had a phone call to make, but not on the public telephone network.

He did not return home but walked fast to an anonymous little flat on the ground floor of an old Franco-era apartment block. It had no name or number. Inside were three bare rooms with no furniture except a table and kitchen chair. From under a floorboard he extracted a large brick-shaped telephonic device with a separate aerial which he clipped into place.

He put through an encrypted call to a certain number in Vauxhall Cross, London, and gave a brief report.

He then sat there for quite a while, worrying about his old friend and colleague Gillian Dams, hoping against hope that she was alright.

He sighed. Being a double agent, and pretending all the time to be as thick as two short planks, was a wearing business.

CHAPTER NINE

Inspector Neish had assembled his team in the small conference room once again.

"Detective Constable Mayne will now bring us all up to date. Thank you, one and all, for your exhaustive efforts to establish contact details for the entire audience on the 20th of October. One of these is proving to be of interest, a young employee of an organ-building firm in Bristol, and not a local. He is a possible suspect in this intricate plot to kill, and as will be explained by Jonathan Mayne, he murdered the wrong person – we think.

"Over to you, Mayne."

And the DC reported the findings to date and the scenario that he had deduced. At last, they seemed to be onto something. This young organ-builder, Henry Newby, had made the classic error of many crooks, in returning to the scene of the crime to see if it would be successful. Overconfidence, and a naive assumption that he would be overlooked as a bona fide member of the audience with a professional interest in a fine organ, had prompted him to give the police his real name and address, no doubt nervous that fake details would be a mistake and lead to immediate suspicion if checked.

This was Mayne's theory, at any rate.

*

Henry Newby had taken his place in a pew halfway down the nave, a couple of minutes before Sir John Winnersley had begun his recital. Newby had found difficulty in finding somewhere to park his MGB, and in the end had to put up with a roadside space right down by the railway station. By the time he had walked fast up Rigby Road to the abbey Close, he was almost late. The fussy verger had frowned at him and hustled him quite unnecessarily to his seat.

This is it, he thought, as he settled on the hard oak pew. If this works, I get my ten thousand pounds from that oddball continental outfit. And if their enemy Miss Gillian Dams plays right through her recital without once drawing the four-foot Tromba, I will have failed and I get nothing. But I would like to see if my little device actually works, he mused.

He was a strange young man.

The vicar, Canon Haskins, had appeared at the chancel steps, and the subdued rumble of conversation immediately ceased. He held up his hands to encourage silence, and spoke his introduction.

"As many of you will know," he said, "our recitalist this evening has undergone a multiple metamorphosis through a series of unrelated circumstances." (A light titter sprinkled itself through the audience from those locals who had noticed the various edited versions of the advertising poster.)

"We were in danger of having to cancel," the Canon continued, "but at the last minute our own dear Sir John, one-time organist of Canterbury Cathedral and now a much-respected resident of this town in his retirement, has graciously offered to save the day.

"A round of applause, please, for… Sir John Winnersley."

Enthusiastic clapping, and a few cheers, had followed this announcement, as the Canon took his seat.

Henry Newby froze. A cold shiver then ran down his spine as he sat there in mute horror. He stared unseeing at the back of the neck of the elderly grey-haired gentleman sitting in the pew ahead.

What should he do? Stand up and stop the proceedings? Explain that the recitalist would, if not careful, get it in the back of the neck?

He stared again at the neck in front of him – an obvious, accusing sort of neck. Newby felt sick.

Sir John had then begun to play, a quiet piece on flutes and a Stopped Diapason.

The Spaniards had assured Newby that the object was to scare, not kill. Miss Dams was a young, healthy girl and the poison dart would knock her out, but she would recover. No, the purpose was to demonstrate to the British authorities that their agents in Gibraltar were up against a sophisticated state campaign with unusual resources.

But now, thought Henry Newby, what about this Sir

John Winnersley? The vicar had said he was in retirement, so he must be quite old. What if he didn't survive?

I may be a murderer. But play safe, play safe. Act normally and look innocent.

Newby had sat there in the abbey for almost the entire recital, that evening of the 20th of October. Rigid from head to foot, he held his breath at every opening of the swell pedal, every thumbing of the next combination piston, every entry into a crescendo.

He had been too late arriving to get a programme. At each closing sequence, each final rallentando, he had breathed a sigh of relief, poised for the next opportunity for the recitalist to shoot himself in the neck.

And then, the opening bars of the Schoenberg. Newby knew this piece, a huge challenge for any organist. He also knew how it ended. Full organ, with all the trimmings. The chorus of Trumpet stops drawn on the Choir department, shining splendidly on its opening swell pedal through the full Diapason chorus and Mixtures on the Great, and supported in a stupendous dissonant chord on the Bombarde section of the pedal department.

A fabulous sound. A certain killer.

Henry Newby got up and left the abbey.

CHAPTER TEN

The 5th of November. Early in the evening, as Canon Haskins sat at his study desk musing over his draft sermon for Sunday's morning service for All Saints, he could see the sporadic trajectory of rocket fireworks beyond the town, bursting into colourful stars over the rooftops and drifting away eastwards in the light breeze.

Suddenly his desk phone rang, shattering in its urgency the meditative silence of the room.

He blinked himself back into the present moment and picked up the handset.

"It's Gillian here, Ben," he heard with a tremor of surprise. "I am so sorry not to have been in touch before, and I owe you my utmost apologies. You must have all been wondering where I had vanished to."

"Gill, my dear, am I relieved to hear your voice," the Canon blurted out. "Are you OK? What on earth happened?"

"Well, I'd better start from the beginning. As you know, I was called away and couldn't practise or commit to giving the recital on the 20th, although I had fully intended to be there on the night to welcome Thomas Canterer – I mean Sir John Winnersley. However, on the morning of the recital I had a call from London which was – um – well, which was a private emergency and I literally had to drop everything and run. Since then I've been overseas and in no position to get in touch till now. But I'm back, and I'm fine."

"But Gillian," the Canon protested, "was this a family crisis abroad, or what? Your life outside the abbey has always been a complete mystery to me. You shouldn't just vanish, you know. I have a responsibility for you as an abbey employee, as well as a Christian duty as a friend and colleague."

There was a silence on the end of the telephone.

"I know, Ben," murmured Gillian Dams in a subdued voice. "It's very difficult, and I wish it were simpler. But there are… um… circumstances involved which I have to keep to myself.

"One of my reasons for phoning is, again with huge apologies, to say that sadly I cannot return to the abbey as organist for the foreseeable future, and it is only fair to you and all my choir colleagues to offer my resignation as of now.

"The fact is, I have this other responsibility which has now become an unavoidable obligation. More than that I can't say."

The vicar and organist exchanged a few pleasantries in some embarrassment and confusion, and hung up as the conversation petered out.

Canon Haskins sat back in his chair and frowned deeply. He had been doing a lot of this recently.

Well, he thought to himself, I don't know, this is all very strange. And she never mentioned the tragedy of poor Sir John, which has been in all the papers and remains a complete mystery.

Anyone would think, he hazarded, that Gillian Dams was some sort of undercover official, what with this cloak-and-dagger secrecy. Oh, well. We shan't ever know, I suppose.

*

The following morning, Inspector Neish called DC Mayne into his office.

"Just had Canon Haskins on the phone. Miss Dams is safe and well, location unknown. He outlined a phone conversation he had with her last night. All consistent with her being with SIS. She's not returning to her abbey job. My guess is that she is back in the thick of it with the Gibraltar situation. There was more in the paper this morning – the Spanish government warning the British ambassador in Madrid that mutual relations would suffer over the Rock unless sovereignty was seriously discussed at Foreign Secretary level.

"Anyway, we can forget Gillian. Our job is to find and arrest a killer. This young Newby fellow will have gone to ground. I want you to go up to Bristol and talk to his employers at that organ-builders.

"Strictly to assist with our enquiries, mind. They may be in on it as far as we know, but I doubt it. We just want to speak to their employee Newby about 'an incident'. OK?"

Jonathan Mayne set off for Osmundson & Rushworthy's works.

The exterior of the drab steel-framed industrial unit belied the jewel box of its interior. As Mayne opened the door into a small reception area, the aroma of freshly sawn hardwoods, the warm smell of worked soft metals and the ethereal flutey sounds of pipe ranks being test-tuned, all hit him in the face as a wave of timeless specialist craftsmanship. A modern intrusion was the steady hum of dust extraction fans and their steel flues suspended in several places from the iron roof frames of the building.

In one corner was the half-dismembered skeleton of an oak organ case, clearly of some elderly vintage, all its innards removed and distributed carefully nearby and sprouting little white luggage labels annotating their sequence and position when reinstated inside the instrument.

Mayne caught the eye of an oldish man in shirt sleeves and grubby white carpenter's apron, who laid down his bottle of button polish and strolled towards him with an enquiring eye.

"The boss, sir?" the man anticipated. "Just one moment and I'll fetch him. He's gluing up some key ivories down the far end." He padded off.

Mayne's attention was suddenly diverted by a very loud, deep sound that reminded him of a lighthouse foghorn. It was closely followed by several others rising in scale a tone apart, one or two notes repeated at short intervals. The astonishing sound came from another corner of the workshop, where an equally elderly man was pressing keys on a rudimentary keyboard structure on which was mounted a rank of gleaming pipes with conical tops, which Mayne recognised as a sixteen-foot stop from one of the Oboe family of organ sounds. With his other hand the operative was tapping the tuning wire of each pipe to tune them as he played their note.

A tall, lanky man of about sixty appeared around the corner of a small organ case, this one also evidently Victorian, but all complete as far as Mayne could see. It had no pedal board, and just one manual, the case front pipes clearly dummy and of painted wood, revealed through two framed oval openings in the immaculate woodwork. A brass plate above the console was inscribed 'Bishop and Son 1856'.

Charlie Draper, proprietor of the firm, introduced himself and raised a bushy eyebrow when Mayne reciprocated with his police rank.

He led him outside, away from the noise and distraction.

The detective constable began. "We are hoping to speak to an employee of your firm, Mr Henry Newby. We believe that he could help us with our enquiries concerning an incident back in late October. Unfortunately we do not have his home address, and so I have called on you in case you can help me with his whereabouts."

"Yes, well, Officer, I can certainly tell you where he lives, but you won't find him at home. He phoned me about a week ago to say that a family tragedy meant he had to rush up to Harrogate and didn't know when he would be able to return to work.

"He certainly sounded in a bad way, poor fellow. I've heard nothing from him since but haven't liked to phone him.

There's no urgency from our point of view. He is working on that rather nice 1897 Walker instrument in there, but a couple of weeks or so won't matter to us or the client.

"A useful young man, that Henry. I have high hopes that he may become a permanent member of staff here. We badly need young blood, as you will no doubt have noticed."

Draper went on to explain, at Mayne's prompting, how Newby had turned up out of the blue to learn the organ-builders' craft.

Mayne made a note of his home address, and on a whim asked to see the references which Newby had provided. Then, after noting down Newby's mobile phone number from Mr Draper's office record, he departed.

First stop was a ground-floor flat in a modern block in Stapleton on the north-east edge of Bristol. As he had easily assumed, Mayne found it empty, his ringing of the bell unanswered. He peered through the front windows but could see no signs of an occupant at home.

He then tried Newby's mobile number. 'Number not recognised'. Why am I not surprised? Mayne asked himself.

He returned south, back to his police station.

The following day he had a response to his enquiry of the British Institute of Organ Studies. They had never heard of Henry Newby and had certainly never provided anyone with a reference for such a person.

Harrogate, eh? sighed Jonathan Mayne. Mr Henry Newby was as likely to be in Harrogate as in any other English town, or continental Europe for that matter.

One last straw to clutch. He accessed the DVLA and police systems for tracing motor vehicles and tried to match an MGB in racing green, registration number unknown, with a Mr Henry Newby.

There were fourteen Henry Newbys as registered keepers of a vehicle currently taxed and on the road, with a valid MOT. Of course, Henry's MGB would be old enough for certain exemptions, but not registration.

None looked remotely promising.

CHAPTER ELEVEN

'WINNERSLEY DEATH – MURDER CONFIRMED' screeched the bold black headline in the *Daily Telegraph*, albeit on page two. (The front page was still devoted to the cost-of-living crisis and the flapping of hands by government ministers.)

This copy of the *Telegraph* was crumpled but still open at page two. The chief from the Lancashire Fire and Rescue service could see it clearly through the crazed hood window of the MGB, which he had reached with difficulty down the almost sheer side of the riverbank.

The battered nose of the green sports car was already half buried in the silt of the fast-flowing current, the windscreen shattered and the dashboard littered with shards of glass.

Both doors were shut. The fire officer and his colleague manoeuvred the aluminium escape ladder a little along the mudbank until he could reach out for the driver's side-door handle. It was completely jammed. The window of the door had misted up on the inside, but peering in as best he could, the officer could make out a black-haired head slumped against the steering wheel, one hand still gripping the wheel rim.

There were no obvious signs of blood, but the head was very still. Dead or unconscious?

Suddenly the car gave a lurch and sank another foot or so into the water, dislodging the firemen's ladder which settled again at an awkward angle.

"Quick, George, get back up and fetch the jemmy and a hydraulic wrench. Get the lads up there to drop another ladder alongside, and the stretcher tackle. Have the paramedics arrived yet? We will want a stretcher and straps and use the ladder as a slide."

His colleague scrambled back up the bank to the shiny red fire tender on the roadside above, its blue lamps flaring in mad syncopation through the murk of an early dawn.

The chief reached for his tried and trusted Musto serrated marine blade and ripped a long cut through the top of the black fabric hood top of the MGB. Another jagged swipe at right angles and he was able to pull open a large flap and look down inside. With some relief he noted that there appeared to be no distortion to the interior structure of the car. The driver, a youngish man, did not seem to be trapped or wedged.

There was no passenger.

The fire officer managed to lean right in and release the driver's seat belt, which was one of those designs popular in 1970s sports circles with dual shoulder straps and a central buckle at chest height. Supremely effective in such circumstances.

Now he could detect a smear of blood at the top of the steering wheel where the man's forehead had clearly impacted with some force. Hurry up, lads, we've got to get this chap out and into recovery if we can, he thought.

*

Two days later, the huge crane had hauled the remains of the MGB out of the river and onto a flatbed truck, which took it initially to the police compound. No documents had been found in it, but Lancashire Police had traced its registered keeper to an Anthony Johnstone at an address in Yeovil, Somerset. He was eighty-six years of age, and had been infirm for more than a decade. From a brief and courteous visit by two Avon and Somerset Police constables it was established that he had kept the car out of pure nostalgia, and had it insured for both himself and his stepson, one Henry Newby – who to all intents and purposes was now its only driver.

Mr Johnstone was devastated to learn that his beloved car was now a complete write-off but certainly most relieved to learn that his stepson Henry was recovering well from his injuries in the Royal Preston Hospital.

All of this information duly reached the laptop of Inspector Neish. Constable Mayne having cleared things with Lancashire Police, the two of them set out for Fulwood to interview the hospital patient as soon as the ward sister permitted them to do so.

*

"You may go in now," the competent and matronly sister announced, some two hours after Neish and Mayne had drawn into the hospital car park and followed the directions from reception to the ward in which Henry Newby lay. "He has suffered a severe frontal head trauma and is still sedated, gentlemen, so please go easy as he will have a significant headache."

Nothing like the headache he will have when we have a prosecution for murder, thought Mayne.

"And no more than twenty minutes," emphasised the nursing sister crisply.

Neither police officer was in uniform, and Newby turned his head, wincing as he did so, with a puzzled frown. They did not look like doctors.

Inspector Neish opened proceedings. "Mr Henry Newby?" he enquired formally, to which Newby gave a cautious nod.

"I am Police Inspector Neish and this is my colleague Detective Constable Mayne. We have a few questions to ask you in connection with an incident in Aldhelm Abbey on the evening of the 20th of October."

Henry Newby did a double-take, clearly visible to the officers as his expression changed. His immediate reaction to their announcing themselves had been the assumption that they were there because of his road accident two days previously. But the 20th of October? That was weeks ago.

Then in a fraction of a second it hit him. He blanched and closed his eyes, slumping his shoulders onto the pillow behind him.

"You were in the audience for an organ recital in the

abbey that evening, I understand?"

Again, Newby nodded.

"We would like to know if you had entered the abbey on a prior occasion and had interfered in any way with the mechanism of the organ up in the gallery."

"In the Choir organ case behind the bench," Jonathan Mayne contributed, wishing to demonstrate that they knew what they were talking about.

Newby lifted his head and looked directly at the detective constable, focusing for the first time on the officer.

Silence. For about ten seconds he held his gaze and said nothing.

"The four-foot Tromba stop?" Mayne continued. "Substitution of a pipe in its windway hole with a mechanism intended as a weapon? We understand that you are an operative with the firm of Osmundson & Rushworthy in Bristol, and are competent in the maintenance of pipe organs."

Henry Newby closed his eyes and lay back on the bed.

"I had better tell you the whole story, I guess," he croaked. "There's more to this than meets the eye. I'm just a small cog in a large machine, but I will tell you all I know."

"That will be wise, Mr Newby," confirmed Inspector Neish.

*

A generous twenty minutes later, the two police officers emerged from the private ward and paused in the corridor.

"Mayne," the inspector murmured, "get onto the local police and ask for a senior officer to phone me on my mobile. Now Newby is under arrest we need a PC on duty outside the ward door, but from what we have learned I am worried he may be got at by his paymasters if they discover where he is. He needs a protection officer as well as a guard. They will be nervous that he could lead us into the heart of their political conspiracy.

"Those premises in Berkeley Square, for instance. What I will do now is get back to the Super and pass on that information so that he can alert SIS at Vauxhall Cross. That's their business, not ours."

"Will do, sir." And they went their separate ways.

CHAPTER TWELVE

The King's Chapel below the towering Rock of Gibraltar was filling up, as dignified army, navy and air force personnel in full uniform filed in and took their places in the pews. A low murmur of courteous conversation formed a background hum to the quiet voluntary being played on the modest little pipe organ at the rear of the nave. The organist himself was in uniform, a young man in the blue and gold of lieutenant commander, hidden from view by the panelled screen behind his bench.

The front few rows had been reserved for the Governor's party and a few senior officers, but otherwise it was a random sea of service colours, with 'other ranks' tending by assumption and long practice to congregate towards the rear. Up near the altar at the east end sat the Chapel Singers, some in uniform but the rest (mainly the sopranos and altos) in civilian dress. A string quartet had somehow been found the space to sit with their instruments and music stands in the chancel.

Thirty seconds to eleven o'clock, and the drone of conversation petered out, everyone present being by long training and experience acutely conscious of precise time-keeping.

By now there was standing room only. A huddle of sailors, airmen and soldiers had gathered just inside the open west doors, about half a dozen. All six had been fully briefed.

Slightly behind this group and standing up against the open door each side of the imposing entrance stood two military policemen, both in civilian clothes.

The organist drew the four-foot Principal, and the Governor with his wife strode with aplomb and authority from the side door out of their quarters, across the nave aisle and into their allotted seats in the front pew. His uniform was magnificent, if smelling slightly of mothballs, its opportunities for display rather infrequent these days.

At the same moment, a modest and easily ignored lance corporal in ordinary field uniform slipped through one side of the west door and stood meekly beside the door jamb, at the very rear of the standing congregation.

The lieutenant commander glanced into his mirror and noted the short nod in his direction from the chaplain at the chancel step. He improvised a graceful conclusion to his voluntary, cancelled his drawn stops and switched off the blower, remaining in his place on the organ bench during the chaplain's welcoming words, and then quietly slipping down to an empty place at the end of the nearest pew.

From this point on, until the final recessional voluntary, his job was done and the musical accompaniment would be provided by the quartet, augmented by two clarinets in amongst the choir.

The first hymn tune was played over, and the service began.

*

It was not quite the loud 'bang' that Mario had been to led to expect. During the last verse of the third hymn, as the chaplain got up from his seat in preparation for his progress to the pulpit for his sermon, he heard a low 'hiss' emanating from the organ, followed by the first wisp of a bright orange smoke curling out of the back of the organ itself.

Mario, of course, was all keyed up to await his cue from a smoke bomb in the gallery, but no one else appeared to notice this orange stuff percolating out from behind the wooden panelling.

I suppose this is it, he thought to himself, and waited a further second or two before reaching down into the front of his camouflage trousers and grasping the solid object suspended in his underpants. He felt for the butt and slowly extracted the weapon, hiding it with both hands over his crotch.

This isn't going to plan, he thought in some panic. Where's the uproar and confusion to distract attention?

The orange smoke was now thicker, and one or two members of the congregation were beginning to look sideways towards the organ case.

Now or never, shrugged Mario. He raised his right arm holding the automatic pistol, but it was no more than waist high when both his arms were seized in an iron grip from behind, and simultaneously his right wrist was agonisingly twisted downwards by a muscular hand in a pale blue uniformed sleeve that had flashed out from the man alongside him.

The pistol fell from his numbed fingers onto the chapel floor. His arms were jerked roughly behind his back and steel handcuffs snapped far too tightly onto his wrists.

The group of men around him closed ranks as a screen from the rest of the congregation, and Mario was hauled out silently, and unresisting, through the west entrance and out into the street, where stood a police van parked by the curb, and into which he was bundled.

*

Mario's erstwhile confederate had carried out his instructions from Madrid, having alerted the British authorities to the planned incident in the King's Chapel. Neither he nor the British Secret Service wished to blow his cover; it had taken years to infiltrate and build trust with the Spanish services.

He had picked up the smoke bomb apparatus from a Madrid contact as intended, and had duly installed it on top of the wind reservoir within the organ the previous day, setting the timer for 11:30 the following morning. For some weeks he had worked diligently as a cleaner in the company used by the Governor's administration, and would continue to do so for another few weeks, all as arranged.

However, at ten o'clock on Sunday, an hour before the chapel service was to begin, a bomb disposal member of the Royal Engineers had called at the chapel in civilian clothes and had quietly gained access to the organ. In a matter of minutes he had substituted the smoke bomb for a small yacht distress flare, leaving the timer mechanism in place.

He had then installed himself behind the organ case, hidden from view, and having allowed the orange flare to hiss away for the few seconds after 11:30am necessary for the Spaniard Mario to be disarmed over at the west door, had simply capped the flare and put it out.

It was doubtful whether more than a dozen members of the congregation ever noticed anything amiss.

The Governor himself could not resist a quick glance back as the incident was so efficiently dealt with, and he allowed himself the gubernatorial equivalent of a smirk.

*

Certain individuals within state departments in Madrid, and the national press contacts that they had lined up, waited in vain for the reports to come through of an attempt on the British Governor's life, and the armed services' panic on Gibraltar that Sunday morning.

CHAPTER THIRTEEN

A large and shiny clean van stood on the tarmac at the west end of St Aldhelm's Abbey, its identity dignified by the lettering on its side reading 'Harrison & Harrison Organ Builders'.

Two of its staff carefully unloaded from the rear a new oak organ bench, a rackboard and feet, and some wooden case panels.

The Reverend Canon Haskins stood in the doorway of his vicarage opposite and watched them with satisfaction.

That's a pleasing sight, he said to himself; another few days and we'll have the abbey filled once again with that glorious sound. All we need is a new organist. I wonder what our Gillian is up to now. That was all very odd. Oh, well. Onwards and upwards.

An early mid-December snowfall had silently blanketed the abbey Close buildings overnight, adhering to the branches of the limes and the great beech in picturesque fashion. Indeed, Ben Haskins spotted a keen photographer leaning against the Close wall, laden with cameras and bristling with lenses like telescopes. No doubt his efforts would shortly be gracing the pages of a glossy county magazine and featuring on postcards in all the gift shops and newsagents for miles around. Perhaps he could be persuaded to negotiate with the Canon a special rate for Christmas cards. A bit late for this year.

The vicar shivered in the cold draught of the doorway, and returned indoors to his morning coffee and sermon writing.

*

After a while, he fell to musing over the recent events that had taken the quiet, gentle life of his abbey church by storm. He had read in his *Times* that an arrest had been made and a man prosecuted and remanded in custody for murder, way up in Lancashire for some reason.

A bitter irony was that dear old Sir John Winnersley, bless him, had long ago bequeathed in his will a very substantial sum in trust for the future preservation and maintenance of the Gray & Davison organ in the abbey. There cannot be many examples, the vicar imagined, of a murder victim donating many thousands of pounds for the upkeep of the weapon that had killed him.

Least of all for a weapon on which the victim had, himself, literally pressed the button for his own demise.

This was all privileged information, of course. The Canon had gleaned as much from two personal sources in recent weeks: one a friend of his who had supervised the clean-up operation in the organ gallery after the Porton Down team had finished poking around up there; and the second a secretary in the coroner's office after the inquest into Sir John's death – a secretary who also happened to be the vicar's daughter.

He had been sworn to secrecy, naturally. He had not been slow to realise that Sir John had hardly been the intended victim. That was much more likely to have been Thomas Canterer or Gillian Dams, simply because of the time needed for the organ mechanism to be tampered with, on the details of which the vicar had no information. The weapon would surely have been triggered by anyone playing the organ and using the Tromba stop anytime after it was set up, presumably some days before the recital on the 20th of October.

Much more likely, therefore, to have been meant for his regular organist, Miss Dams.

But why? If she was undercover as some kind of Secret Service agent, maybe she had been a target in some international conspiracy. She had survived that attempt, but was her life still under threat?

Such a beautiful girl, too, he thought. He was only human.

CHAPTER FOURTEEN

At precisely the same time as Canon Haskins' mind was wandering from his sermon preparation that morning, the girl so closely matching the image in his mind's eye was walking purposefully into Berkeley Square in London with a large shopping bag.

It was a chilly morning and Gillian had on a close-fitting padded jacket, cord trousers and a thick, woolly hat drawn down over her ears. The jacket was done up with metallic buttons, the topmost button containing the lens of a small digital video camera zipped into the back of the padding. This device also recorded close-up sound via a tiny microphone in the second button down.

Sewn into the large bobble on her hat was a miniature PLB, a locator beacon on a restricted wavelength reserved by the Secret Intelligence Service, MI6, not so very far away in Vauxhall Cross.

She then wandered into the oval park amongst the ancient plane trees and sat on a bench. Her instructions followed statements and interviews by the police with Henry Newby, who had described the premises and their access in which he had downloaded his design for weaponising the organ at St Aldhelm.

These were in Hill Street, just off the square, and his key and password were in Gillian's pocket.

Having sat for a while and satisfied herself that no individual in her field of vision had been hovering suspiciously in surveillance, she promptly stood and walked with an air of confident routine straight across into Hill Street and, without hesitating, into a dark tarmac access to a sloping ramp that led down to a car park beneath one of the prestigious office buildings lining the street.

The concrete basement was essentially a garage, accommodating about twenty vehicles, many of which were pristine, shiny, outsize 4x4s with darkened window glass, the standard commuting conveyances from outer London suburbs for the bright young executives working in the offices on the floors above.

They did have one feature in common that worked to Gillian's benefit, that of height and breadth, enabling her to negotiate, by ducking low, the distance into the dimly lit corner where the short flight of steps rose up to a steel door with an intercom. No one appeared to be in the garage at that moment, to her relief.

She walked calmly up the steps and spoke Newby's password into the microphone unit on the wall. The door clicked open and in she went.

No one was in the corridor. Under the vicious glare of fluorescent strip lights, her heart thumping in percussive accompaniment to the deep, heavy hum of some powerful hidden equipment, she counted the doors along the passage and inserted Newby's key into the lock of the room that he had occupied.

Twisting the door handle, she pushed the door open and reached automatically for the light switch.

In a millisecond she realised that the room was already lit up. Seated at the grey metal desk, facing away from the doorway and muffled with a set of thick earphones, was a man intently gazing at a green computer screen and tapping away at his keyboard.

Gillian froze where she stood, but after a couple of seconds that felt like light years, she realised that he was unaware of her clandestine entrance.

She had been well trained. Her SIS initiation had included three months with the SAS. She not only knew how to defend herself but had also learned the art of incapacitating a target into unconsciousness, with pressure accurately applied behind the ear simultaneously with the smothering of nose and mouth with a thick pad clamped forcibly onto the face with the other hand.

The pad was one item of several useful articles contained in her large shopping bag.

The man at the desk slumped forward without a sound, and Gillian lowered him gently to the floor, taking his place in the office chair.

She smiled to herself. The computer was open and active, offering unrestricted access to some programs, if not all. Hacking would not be required.

She took a memory stick from her pocket and plugged

it into the USB port. A further thought occurred to her, and she returned briefly to the door of the room, locking it on the inside and leaving the key lodged in the keyhole.

Taking her seat once again, she set to work downloading as much as she could find from the programs and the hard drive.

It did not take long. The man at her feet began to show signs of recovering consciousness. She pressed 'eject' and unplugged the memory stick. Dropping it into a pocket, she regained on screen the program he had been working on, silently rose from the chair and tiptoed to the door, which mercifully unlocked without a sound. Slipping out into the passageway, she re-locked the door.

With a bit of luck, the operative in the room would awake in the belief that he had inexplicably fainted on duty.

Glancing both ways along the corridor, Gillian retraced her steps to the heavy entrance door.

Only then did she notice that above the door frame a CCTV camera lens stared down at her, the little green light on its case blinking like a pulse.

The big exit button, exactly the same shape and size of an organ stop-knob, released the door instantly, and she departed like a wraith through the parked commuter tanks and out into Hill Street.

Once again, she knew that she was a marked woman, easily identifiable, recorded somewhere on a digital CCTV film.

CHAPTER FIFTEEN

"Henry Newby," demanded the judge in the Winchester Crown Court room, "would you stand, please.

"You pleaded guilty to the charge of murder and it is my duty to pronounce sentence accordingly. The court has heard argument for mitigation from your barrister Mr Rumbold, and I am minded to acknowledge that there was no intent in regard to the actual unfortunate victim, Sir John Winnersley, whose death in that respect was an accident of circumstance.

"Nonetheless, you acted voluntarily, and with a motive of financial gain, as an agent for an organisation with which you had no other connection, the identity of which is of no relevance to this case. I accept that you have provided helpful information to the authorities in that respect.

"It has been claimed on your behalf that you were led to believe that the toxin which you were supplied would cause injury but not death. I reject that as mitigation – the risk involved would have been dependent upon the health of the intended victim, on which you had no information whatever.

"Your careful, premeditated and purposeful adaptation of the organ mechanism was a conscious and callous act of gratuitous assault.

"I am obliged in law to impose on you a sentence of life imprisonment. This is in practice subject to what is known as a tariff, which means the minimum period that you will serve in custody. Now, the minimum tariff in a case involving a firearm or explosive is thirty years. I have given due consideration as to whether the wickedly ingenious, and no doubt unique, weapon you devised can be deemed to constitute a firearm, and have determined that it is not.

"You are entitled to a discount for your early guilty plea, and taking into account all aggravating and mitigating factors, I am sending you to prison today for a minimum term of eighteen years."

*

Inspector Neish and Detective Constable Mayne stood on the steps of Winchester Court.

"Well, sir," said Mayne, "that's us done then. Back to shoplifting and petty fraud, I suppose. Hey ho."

"Yes, you did well, Mayne. If you had not been a church organist and knowledgeable about those extraordinary church instruments, we would have got nowhere."

"Oh, thank you, sir. Chapel organist in my case, being a dyed-in-the-wool nonconformist."

"Hmm. Try not to be too nonconformist, at any rate when in uniform."

*

Two other individuals slipped out of the court some moments later, having observed the proceedings from the public gallery.

Neither were known to the other. One was a man in his thirties, in a bland blue business suit and with an eminently forgettable appearance that was accustomed to merging almost invisibly into a crowd and out again without anyone giving him the slightest attention. He walked quietly away towards the railway station bound for London, and a short walk back to his office in Vauxhall Cross.

The other observer had been a woman of sharp and distinguished features, black-haired and immaculately elegant in a classical Hispanic fashion. She too was headed back to London, to her embassy address in Chesham Place, just off Belgrave Square.

Both were relieved and grateful that the Crown Court judge, in her wisdom, had kept her sentencing pronouncement remarks limited and brief, omitting all reference to the wider issue of intended victim and institutional motive. The CPS prosecutor had been instructed to avoid any such identification in his presentation of the case, an instruction that had come down from those heights of authority that draw thick black bars of redaction through public documents 'in the interests of national security'.

*

Meanwhile, Gillian had returned to her safe house south of the Thames and had, as instructed, downloaded the memory stick onto her secure SIS laptop for initial analysis.

With her was a colleague who was a specialist in Spanish national affairs and a fluent bilingual.

For three hours they worked their way through the data. Much of it concerned detailed plans for disruption of political, military and civil life on Gibraltar: reports, contacts, connections, stolen drawings of secure government premises, timings and itineraries of senior British personnel and of naval vessels; a comprehensive and alarming range of information in the hands of those intent on mischief on a grand scale.

Gillian and her colleague took a break to consider the general picture and wider implications of this initial trawl through the content of the Hill Street computer.

"You know," said Gillian with a thoughtful frown, "there's something not quite right here. Where are the links and references to the Spanish secret services that are already familiar to us? Don't you get the impression that this whole initiative is somehow self-contained; out on a limb?"

"I see what you mean," he replied. "There are links with individuals, rather random, within Madrid government departments, and incidentally within their embassy here in London; but not via the internal mainstream government routes, which of course we have known for years.

"And, Gill," he realised aloud, "the whole tone of what we have read just now is over-excited, a bit defensive –

anarchic, even. If this is official Spanish government activity, would it not be far more laidback and measured? Spanish bureaucracy is entirely missing here."

Gillian stood and stretched. She had sat on her office chair for too long.

"We need to fix a conflab at 85 Albert with 'C'. If we have unearthed an internal civil conspiracy within the politics of Spain, which may include individuals within government and embassy staff, this is a severe diplomatic issue that needs alerting at the highest level.

"My instructions are to stay put here, as I am on their hit list. But you take the memory stick, Patrick, and get back to base PDQ and fix a meeting with the chief."

CHAPTER SIXTEEN

A week later, the Spanish ambassador was invited to the Foreign, Commonwealth and Development Office on a matter of interest to both parties. The Foreign Secretary, who like many of her immediate predecessors had only been in post for five months, hosted the meeting with the quiet confidence of one who could rely totally on the briefing and murmured guidance of her Permanent Under-Secretary, Sir Robyn.

She had reason to be hospitable, and had ordered a cafetière of proper coffee and a plate of the best offerings from Carrs of Carlisle. Over the previous days, MI6 had been busy energising its web of connections in western European extremities. An alarming picture had emerged: a massively funded intrigue right under the noses of the Spanish government.

The Kingdom of Spain had for some years been keen to normalise relationships with the Kingdom of Morocco, a few miles on the opposite shore of the Strait of Gibraltar.

Diplomatic connections had been strained by dispute over entitlement to control of regions of the Western Sahara, its roots dating back to the time that Morocco was part of the Spanish empire. There was increasing goodwill on both sides, at the highest level.

Then in recent years a menace to this relationship had emerged from the distant east. The totalitarian state of China had begun to dig its tentacles into the investment and trade opportunities of the continent of Africa.

China began to see Morocco as a strategic location. Not only did it begin to develop closer economic ties, and their consequent influence on Moroccan affairs, but the Chinese also saw the country as one of the gateposts to the entrance into the entire Mediterranean Sea, a powerful potential geo-political feature.

The other gatepost was Spain, a Western power with political weight through the rest of Europe, strategic anathema to the interests of Chinese expansionism.

This gatepost needed undermining and destabilising. China's most fruitful agent in this task was Morocco – officially or unofficially.

And so, insidious undercover moves, funded by China, began to creep into the political structures of Spain, and at lowly level into its governmental workings as well.

What better ruse to help destabilise relations between Spain and the rest of Europe than to start acts of subversion and destructive incidents on Gibraltar as though they were perpetrated on official Spanish government instructions?

*

"Naturally," the Spanish Ambassador nodded to the Foreign Secretary, "my country is aware of the risk of such foreign meddling in our affairs, and we have taken some care in monitoring the most likely routes by which such subversion could emerge."

Silently he was smarting at the satisfied expression on his host's face, and ground his teeth as she went on to explain how her British Secret Services had discovered the individual lowly perpetrators that would no doubt steer the Spanish authorities to their leadership embedded in government circles.

"My government will be grateful to His Majesty's government for this information," the ambassador continued, "without prejudice of course to the official policy of my government concerning sovereignty rights over Gibraltar, which remain unchanged."

With that, accompanied by one more water biscuit, he left the Foreign Office and swore repeatedly at his embassy driver all the way home.

CHAPTER SEVENTEEN

The Rev Canon Ben Haskins alighted from his railway carriage at Waterloo station on a cool, blustery morning, just after the earlier wave of commuter passengers had dissipated in all directions to their places of work in the great metropolis.

Once again it was the season of General Synod of the Church of England, the quasi-parliamentary ruling congregation of the nation's established church. The Canon had been re-elected to its House of Clergy and it was his duty now for three days to listen, vote and, if necessary, rise to speak on any of the solemn issues coming before that august body in its uncomfortable journey that ran parallel to the secular political and social concerns of the country.

Ben Haskins thoroughly enjoyed these breaks in the routine of parish life at home. The Synod debates were sometimes a bit dull, infrequently somewhat contentious and much more often an enjoyable opportunity to sit and observe the diverse characters that made up the membership of this earnest representation of Christian believers.

He arrived too early to stroll along the Embankment and over Westminster Bridge to meet his fellow members of Synod at Church House, and paused outside the station looking for a distraction.

He spotted the diminutive spire of St John's Church, Waterloo, and on a whim decided to go down the hill and take a look.

It was a London church that he had never visited before – a Greek revival edifice built in 1824, its principal external feature being the immense and dignified portico with its six fluted Doric columns serving the west end entrance.

He trotted briskly up the steps and was pleased to see that the doors were open. There was a strong smell of paint, and some piles of dust sheets in the large lobby area. A display board explained that a massive scheme of renovation was just being completed.

The Canon wandered into the main hall, now bathed in light from its white-painted makeover. The green-coloured woodblock flooring was still being restored, but he found a chair beneath the gallery and sat down to contemplate his surroundings.

There was no one else about. He had the hall to himself, it seemed. Sitting there in the silent atmosphere, insulated from the traffic roar outside by the new glazed doors separating hall from narthex, he began to doze.

How long he had been slumbering, he couldn't say. Gradually he realised that something was drawing him up from the depths into consciousness. A sound. Rather a sweet, soft sound – a slow tune, in fact, apparently drifting down from somewhere high above him.

A snatch of Herbert Howells. He recognised it. The tune stopped in mid-bar, and was repeated in a slightly different sound.

Of course! Someone had begun to play the organ in the gallery overhead.

Ben Haskins got up and moved out into the centre of the hall, turning around to gaze up at the elegant organ cases, the main case partially hidden behind the matching Choir organ.

The music began to swell as the organist added upper work and a Mixture. The pedal part was introduced, a steady, deep and penetrating sound that began to fill all four corners of the classical hall space around him, while the bright crystal notes of the upper harmonics soared up to the distant ceiling above and seemed to swirl around that vast volume of space as though confined, wanting to burst out of the building and – now some Trumpet reeds being drawn by the invisible organist – take Waterloo by storm, to drown the pedantic rumble of lorry, bus and railway train in the world beyond.

The Canon was intrigued. He and the organist were alone in this monumental structure. He felt he was a kindred spirit.

The stairs to the gallery ran up from the narthex in the north-west corner. He quietly climbed them and, reaching the top, found that he was looking at the back view of the organist seated at a detached console of a rather 1950s vintage that faced the organ case some distance away at right angles.

He stood still and silently watched and listened.

She was having a bit of difficulty with some of the stops, or perhaps was experimenting with the sounds. One or two stops didn't appear to be working properly. He could sense her frustration.

He spotted a little brass plate screwed to the console case: 'Bishop and Sons. Rebuilt by Hele 1883. Restored Noel Mander 1951.'

Overdue for another restoration job, he thought.

For the first time, he focused on the player. It was chilly, and she wore a puffer jacket with a padded hood that she hadn't folded down fully.

Something vaguely familiar about her dark hair, and her moving figure on the organ bench, rang a bell or two in the Canon's memory.

The organist reached up to turn the page of her score on the music desk. She paused suddenly.

Odd, isn't it, how a sixth sense can tell you that someone you cannot see is watching you?

She swung round on the organ bench and stared.

"Ben?"

"Hello, Gillian." He smiled in reply. "I thought I recognised the handling of Herbert Howells."

"But… what on earth brings you here, Ben? Rather a different world from sleepy St Aldhelm's! I come here sometimes to keep my hand in, as you see. I'm at a bit of a loose end at present, as it happens. They've retired me from the Service, for good behaviour, so I have plenty of free time."

The Canon looked thoughtful.

"Miss Gillian Dams, I have an unfilled vacancy for Abbey Organist at St Aldhelm's. Might you be interested?"

Gillian turned back to the keyboard and thumbed a red piston under the lower key slip. At full organ she nailed a four-octave glissando and a minor seventh over a subdominant on the pedal sixteen-foot Trombone, much to the consternation of an elderly visitor who had just entered the hall below.

"Just try and stop me," she said.

THE MAGISTRATE

A short adventure of kidnap and revenge,
drawing on the work of a Justice of the Peace today.

CHAPTER ONE

It was in my lunch break that I first became conscious of him. He was on the other side of the road at the bus stop. He stared across at me, unblinking.

Now, some people may be under the illusion that in their lunch hour magistrates, or Justices of the Peace, retire to some kind of private dining room in the Law Courts for their meal. Sadly, even the Crown Court judges with whom we share the building have to eat their sandwiches at the desk like ordinary mortals, although I daresay a small glass of Bordeaux might accompany their repast.

As for the magistrates, we could either go down to the reception level and buy an offering from the Diocesan Mothers' Union kiosk so nobly staffed by kindhearted volunteers (dodging the queue of offenders we will be sentencing after lunch) or walk down into town to a sandwich shop.

That is, assuming we get a lunch hour at all. Sometimes the time constraints on progressing cases reduce our break to twenty minutes or so.

At any rate, I was walking briskly that Wednesday in the hot sunshine down to the nice little sandwich bar at St Peters, and there he was, staring at me from across the Milton Road.

He was alone. Slightly scruffy in washed-out blue jeans and a faded tee-shirt bearing the message 'THE ANSWER TO LIFE IS NO' across the chest in black capitals. Head shaved, shinily reflecting the sunlight, in an unsuccessful attempt to hide early-onset baldness. About thirty-five years of age.

Had I seen him before? It was hard to say. I often come home from a sitting in court to be asked by my wife, "Had an interesting day, dear?", to which I am about to describe my cases but find that my mind is a complete blank.

A merciful trait in some ways. The antics and attitudes of many offenders, and the decisions we have taken in court, are best left behind. I know that some of my colleagues wake up in the following small hours anxiously reviewing their judgments or reliving some gory police body camera evidence on the video screen; but with me, the only things that tend to stick around in my head are violence to children or an infuriating administrative failure in the court technology, both of which are all too frequent.

Of course, at that end of the Milton Road a man striding along the pavement in a fine worsted suit by Luscombes, sporting a discreet breast pocket handkerchief, as is my wont, is only too likely to be an object of disbelief to the casual lounger leaning against the bus shelter amongst the flotsam and jetsam of discarded pot noodle packets and lager cans.

At the time, I gave him little further thought as my

mind was still on the intricacies of the trial over which I was presiding, and which had been briefly adjourned for lunch.

It was a nasty case. An allegation of domestic violence prosecuted as Actual Bodily Harm. An earlier court had in its wisdom decided we should keep it, but from what I had heard so far it would have seemed more suitable for passing up to the Crown Court. Still, we could always send it up for sentencing if we found the fellow guilty.

The defendant's word against that of the alleged victim with no other witnesses, as usual. Small children watching wide-eyed and white-faced from the staircase. The woman's face and neck in a bad way, judging from police photographs the following morning. Her partner had a black eye and a bruised shin, but this occasion had prompted the fourth visit from the police on call-outs from neighbours concerned about the shouts and screams over the last three months. The screams had always been female, the shouts angry and male.

I returned from the shop with my ham salad sandwich and apple juice. The bus stop was deserted.

*

A week later I was in Court 3 for remands and general sentencing for those who had pleaded guilty to the usual range of criminal damage, harassment, common assault and shoplifting. There were thirty-two cases on the court listing for the day. The prison van would not arrive until eleven o'clock, and so we needed to press on at ten o'clock with as many other cases we could.

These were, predictably, not very many. Several offenders had not turned up on time, and so the duty defence solicitors were still rushing around behind the scenes with their clients, rapidly piecing together the approach they would take when their client reached the dock. "A little more time, if it pleases your Worships – say ten minutes?"

So my two 'winger' colleagues and I traipse back to the retiring room yet again for a cup of coffee and a grumble.

The legal adviser for the day, hauled in from the Southampton court due to illness, cannot get the computer to do what he wants because the technology is completely different from what he is used to. Our ever-helpful usher is trying to assist him, but the draconian staff cuts in recent years mean that she is ushering in both courts simultaneously that day, and in any case is constantly needing to retreat to her little office to sort out a glitch in the 'cloud' video booking for one of the prisoners on remand, who for some inexplicable reason can be seen on the screen without voice contact.

So we wait, with another cup of instant court coffee. (In the old days we were provided with ground coffee and a percolator, with chocolate biscuits and fresh milk. These days it is a large tin of stale catering-grade Nescafé and little plastic pimples of UHT, of indeterminate date. But I digress.)

It is quite rare to have ordinary interested citizens in the public gallery. Unidentified occupants of those seats are generally family or friends of the accused, or sometimes their victims. Even the press desk is perpetually empty, since the enthusiastic young reporter from the local weekly newspaper moved on to higher things. The only regular attender in the gallery is the volunteer Court Chaplain, his presence offering some reassurance and compassion to one or other occupier of the dock, towards whom he has spent a quarter of an hour exerting his calming influence.

We on the Bench are therefore quite intrigued to study the faces and demeanour of those in the public seats at the back of the courtroom, musing during the gaps in activity what connection each person might have with the little scripted drama of court procedures unfolding before them.

On this occasion, from the moment we processed into court on the dot of ten o'clock and took our little bow to the assembled company, there he was, in the gallery, still in his tatty jeans and loudspeaker tee-shirt.

Still staring directly at me, with very pale blue eyes and an unchanging, impassive expression.

We all took our seats, and I turned my attention to the

job in hand, preparing my words of resigned deprecation for the first of many apologetic requests from the advocates, the usher or the legal adviser to delay progress for one familiar arcane reason or another.

And as usual, we three 'beaks' cast our eyes to the heavens and retreated again 'for no more than ten minutes, your Worships'.

On our eventual return to the bench we were able at last to commence work in earnest. It was twenty-five to eleven. Quite prompt, today.

He never stopped staring at me, trying to engage my eye for the whole morning. He was not interested in any of the cases that came and went with the regularity of a steam engine piston. He ignored my two colleagues completely.

Just before lunch I leant over the desk and murmured to the legal adviser to ask if he knew why the man was there, or whether he knew who he was. No idea. I asked him to get the usher to look in at the retiring room at lunchtime, and I would see if she knew anything about the man.

"Well, sir," she said as I munched my Mothers' Union baguette, "I don't know who he is, but Mark on reception told me that he had asked particularly which court you were sitting in today. He knew your name. I rather supposed he was an acquaintance, or something…" She trailed off. I shook my head and shrugged my shoulders.

"No, I see that's a bit unlikely, sir."

One of my colleagues said she rather thought he was vaguely familiar. That was the problem really. He fitted the mould of any one of hundreds of men frequenting the sleazier parts of town, and of the Law Courts.

At two o'clock we returned to the courtroom. Ten cases to go.

The man in the pessimistic tee-shirt had gone.

*

At quarter past five we finished, turned off and signed back our court iPads (those infuriating objects of digital frustration foisted upon us in recent years), and descended to the private judiciary car park.

For some months the sixteen-foot-high gates, supposedly operated only by our security ID cards, had been jamming open or shut despite several replacement hydraulics, and for everyone's convenience had in the end been left permanently open. They had been open all that day.

I got into my car and dumped my briefcase onto the passenger seat. As I was writing the attendance times into my expenses notebook, I notice a torn slip of paper lodged underneath a wiper blade. I got out again and went around the front of the car to retrieve it.

In pencil was written the words 'I'll be seeing ya' in scrawly handwriting. At the time I smiled to myself, believing it to be one of the little jokes I used to share with the friendly precinct security officer Mike. He and I would swap favourite novels occasionally, and compare notes on which Crown Court judge owned which expensive classy motor car in the reserved parking spaces. (They were mere employees, while we lay JPs were devoted volunteers. Why did we not have the reserved spaces?)

It is only in retrospect that I have fitted that scrappy message into the string of alarming events that were to encircle me over the next few months. Had I made the connection at once, I would have realised that whoever it was with a particular questionable interest in me knew not only my name but my car and its registration number. What else might he have known – my home address, phone number, the name of my wife?

I could then have been better prepared.

Naturally there are established procedures for reporting and dealing with intimidation of the judiciary, including protective measures under police supervision. But being stared at a few times hardly seemed to me to warrant any formal alert.

Later, much too late, I bitterly regretted my initial dismissal of the matter from my mind.

CHAPTER TWO

Towards the end of July a colleague and I were to present a session at one of the secondary schools on the outskirts of the city. This was an hour's worth of structured engagement with the school kids organised by the Magistrates Association as part of their long-established project 'Magistrates in the Community'. Some of us on the Bench offered to take part in the programme annually, and I had done so for at least twenty years. It was very rewarding, encouraging the youngsters to think logically and decide sample cases using the skills of justice: compassion, deterrence, punishment and rehabilitation in appropriate measure, often with results that surprised them. Boys at the fee-paying prep schools tended rather amusingly to focus more on punishment than did their similar year groups at an academy. Grammar-school kids and those from the better comprehensives struck the most measured balance in my experience. The big famous public schools rarely chose to take part.

At any rate, this particular occasion went quite well. The class was of boys and girls approaching their mock GCSEs, and we were part of a 'citizenship day' in which professionals from several agencies made presentations, including the fire service, the police, the NHS trust, the Samaritans and the ambulance service. These had all sparked the interest of the kids and they were in the right mood to engage.

We always start our session by introducing ourselves by our names, what we do or did for our livelihood or career, familiarity with the county, perhaps a word or two about our family – all to get across the message that lay Justices of the Peace are ordinary people, representing (in theory) most aspects and levels of society and ethnic backgrounds, our role – unique anywhere in the world – being that we dispense justice from a personal knowledge and experience of life as lived by those appearing before us. A fine principle, if a little unrealistic. Still, it is more true today than forty years ago, let alone at any time previously.

This session began with my colleague introducing herself, and then it was my turn. Afterwards, I recollected a rather odd reaction from one of the lads as soon as I had given my name.

Up to that point I think he had been as relaxed and smiling as most of his chums. He was sitting near the front and I guess I would have noticed if he had looked particularly glum.

However, as soon as I told the class my name, I saw this boy instantly freeze. He set his mouth in a grim line, and scarcely uttered three syllables for the rest of the session.

He just looked very uncomfortable, and did all he could to avoid eye contact either with me or with my colleague.

Of course, I made no connection at the time with any other odd experience over previous months, let alone the man in Court 3. Why should I have done so?

In retrospect, the reader might think what a pity it was that I did not ask the teacher the name of the boy who had so instantly disengaged. That, however, would have been quite out of the question. The rules of the project, to say nothing of the schools' strict regimes on child-protection measures, prohibit any personal contact with pupils or their identification, and quite right too.

One thing I did remember afterwards, though. This young lad had quite penetrating pale blue eyes.

*

Magistrates have several solo responsibilities outside court. We can countersign firearm licence applications and a wide variety of documents brought to us by individuals. Of particular interest are search warrant applications brought to a single magistrate by a police officer. By their nature they are at short notice, and usually appear as a sideline in the court building, when we fit them into lulls in the listed court hearings.

Sometimes, however, the desired timing of that unexpected knock on the door of a suspect by police officers needs a warrant late in the evening, or at anytime during the night, if the opportunity has arisen unexpectedly.

These days it is usually a court legal adviser who phones

us at home to arrange a personal application, though sometimes a police inspector will get in touch with us directly, having cleared the procedure with a legal adviser on their out-of-hours phone number.

Many a search warrant application has therefore been made before a JP dressed in his or her pyjamas and dressing gown in their kitchen at some unearthly hour, by a police constable dispatched for the purpose. Due formality is attempted, the oath taken, and the information laid, scrutinised, questioned and considered within strict procedural guidelines. Then the magistrate grants the application or declines it.

Declining it (the officer having braved the drenching rain and several hours beyond his shift, and missed his evening at home with the children) can be awkward, but if we are genuinely unconvinced of the case made, then we must do so without hesitation. The oath which we ourselves take on being appointed a JP, to 'do right to all manner of people after the laws and usages of this Realm, without fear, favour, affection or ill will', is fundamentally important and can be contrasted with the ethos imposed on the so-called judiciary in nations around the world of a more totalitarian flavour, which seem to be on the march again.

Well, having now painted the picture I can go on to describe one such occasion that follows this story and which took place in early April, a couple of weeks after our presentation in the school.

I was at home and the telephone rang at about nine-thirty in the evening. I was just taking the dog out into the

garden for her bedtime relief and nosey around the shrubs and trees sniffing for squirrels to bark at.

A legal adviser, John. Could I hear a search warrant application that was urgent? The officer would be with me in about twenty-five minutes. John had already run through the paperwork procedure with the constable and confirmed to me that it was all in order.

"Of course," I replied, "but it's a long way out of town. No luck finding anyone closer?" My wife and I lived way out in the countryside in a tiny village fifteen winding miles from town, five miles indeed from the nearest shop. As a result, these calls rarely came my way.

"Well, sir, the thing is, the search address is only a few miles from the county border, and you happen to be on their route."

"They?" I queried.

"The inspector is coming too, I understand," he replied.

"Heavens, it must be serious." I rang off.

Shortly after ten they duly turned up, and my wife tactfully left us to it around the kitchen table.

It was a common scenario. Class A drug-dealing suspected, with a bit of illicit tobacco importation on the side. All apparently run from a slightly isolated house and garage some miles to the west that was owned, or at any rate occupied, by a Londoner tipped off to the police as a big name in the 'county lines' network of drug traffickers.

Detective constables had been monitoring the premises for a week with binoculars and a camera, and now it was my job to consider whether the reports of suspicious criminal activity at the property justified a search warrant.

It was quite straightforward and convincing. The officers had included two or three photographs in their information.

One of the photos showed the open garage door, revealing stacks of cardboard boxes identified at long range as cartons of cigarette packets identical to some recently intercepted at the docks in Southampton and found to be illegally imported.

In front of the house was a silver Mercedes sports saloon dating from the 1990s, with the back view of two men standing nearby.

The registration number of the car was obscured by shrubbery, but one of the men appeared to be the owner, as he clearly had just got out from the driver's door as the camera clicked.

It was a warm, sunny scene and the shaved pate of this man was reflecting the sunlight.

He was wearing a pair of tatty jeans and a pale, grubby tee-shirt, his top half, turned slightly towards the camera lens, just revealing in black capital letters 'THE ANSW... NO'.

I granted the application and offered the officers a cup of tea, but they declined as they were anxious to seize the moment and do some door-knocking.

"By the way," I asked as they were gathering up their papers, "that chap in the photo with the tee-shirt and jeans. He looks familiar to me. I think I've seen him in the public gallery in court some while ago."

"He's the registered owner of the car, sir, but not the man we're after at the address. We are still making enquiries about the driver of the vehicle."

"You mean you have established the car's registration?"

"Yes, sir. Goodnight then, sir."

Hmm. The inspector was playing it by the book. I was not going to get any more out of him, sadly. Having done my duty, my role had now reverted to that of any other man in the street, an ordinary citizen, without privilege or position.

CHAPTER THREE

Over the next day or two I mused sometimes about this character 'Tee-Shirt', trying to think what possible connection he and I might have had, if any. I dredged my memory yet again for any recollection of a court case in which he may have appeared before me. Nothing sprang to mind, but he could have been one of dozens of visually indistinguishable men in identikit clothing. That is, except for the slogan that he so obviously cherished across his chest. I would surely have remembered that if I had seen him wearing it in the dock.

At least, this was the assumption that I was now beginning to make. Was he an offender with a grievance, happy to spend a few hours of his day trying to intimidate me, for want of anything better to do with his time?

And now (a further assumption) he was evidently mixed up in some nasty business with the heroin dealer over the hill, and so the connection with me seemed ever more likely to be an old court case in which he had appeared;

or perhaps one in which a family member or friend had suffered the weight of justice and had now prompted him to react on their behalf.

Yes, maybe that was it. It would explain the fact that he himself rang no bells with me at all.

*

I next came across him on the forecourt of the Shell filling station near the Law Courts on the Milton Road. This time it was not a deliberate encounter on his part, and in fact he did not spot me.

He was filling petrol into a silver-grey Mercedes that had seen better days. Door sill corrosion and a few dents were now evident. I made a note of its registration number as he roared off with either a dodgy silencer or a souped-up engine. There was a lad in the car with him, presumably his son, clearly in school uniform.

I had just finished a day's sitting in the Youth Court, which deals with offenders and dependents aged ten to seventeen years of age. Technically this court is quite distinct from both the Crown Court and the Magistrates' Court, although its judiciary are only magistrates. I had presided over youth for about ten years and have always found it a little more positive and encouraging in its outcomes than the adult jurisdiction. The focus is on providing for the best interests of the child, in tandem with sentences that are designed to promote a turnaround in attitudes, lifestyle and peer pressure using well-researched structured programmes run by the Youth Offending Teams, the equivalent of adult Probation Services.

Of course, as in so much of the criminal justice system today, ill-informed and counterproductive government policies to minimise expenditure and prioritise 'efficiency' over justice have meant that these rehabilitation and restorative programmes are starved of resources and cannot hope to achieve their potential effectiveness. Nonetheless, they are what they are, and can produce the desired result in many heart-warming cases.

Ultimately, however, there are some young people who pass through the Youth Court time and again with depressing immunity to any of the Youth Offending Teams' efforts. In my experience this is usually because of the total inadequacy of their parents in instilling any moral or societal boundaries in their domestic home life either for themselves or their offspring. A natural life of petty crime can then begin within the chaotic family setting at an early age.

The tragedy that can follow is often inevitable. The child leaves home or is booted out, and the social services step in. The child is placed in a children's home, unloved and bewildered. I have dealt with twelve–and thirteen–year-old offenders who have in their brief childhood and adolescence been accommodated in as many as five children's homes around the country.

They then turn up in court for the umpteenth time for, say, criminal damage and common assault. They have lost their young temper and chucked a stone through a window of the home, and then kicked the shins of a staff member who remonstrated with her or him.

And I say quietly to myself as I listen to this familiar saga in the courtroom, "Quite frankly, who can blame you?"

Regrettably, however, there are some youngsters with whom one has less sympathy. A few are from homes that are reasonably stable and in which it is clear that their parent (generally singular) takes a responsible approach to bringing up children despite daily financial struggles. Up to the age of sixteen, young people up in court must be accompanied by a parent or guardian, who must also attend at least some of the Youth Offender Panel meetings to decide a programme for our sentence under a Referral Order, the first step in the sentencing menu. Failing to accompany their child carries severe sanction.

Unlike the adult Magistrates' Court, the Youth Presiding Justice engages in extensive dialogue with both child and parent during the court hearing, and one soon forms a picture of the conditions, attitudes and relationships that set the domestic scene at home.

Sometimes it is abundantly clear that a parent has done all they can. Their sixteen–or seventeen–year–old daughter or son has been through all the available programmes and sanctions from a string of ever-worsening previous offences, and here they are back in court again, maybe for a burglary or an Actual Bodily Harm. The Youth Offending Team has produced its pre-sentence report which concludes that from their point of view they can only repeat or extend the current programme, with which the teenager has failed to comply satisfactorily anyway.

This leaves us with only one option, a Detention and Training Order. In effect this is imprisonment, within a Young Offenders' Institution. There, the training and rehabilitation element is harder to avoid.

We can imprison young people in this way for up to two years. For adults, our maximum was then six months for one offence (very recently this has been extended to twelve months). A pronouncement of this sentence can come as a major shock to parents, if not to the offender. Tears and outstretched arms towards their child are not uncommon. Quick hugs are given and received in the stunned silence. (The Youth Court has no dock. Offender, parent and defence advocate all sit together.)

Just occasionally, as the parties walk dejectedly out of court, a parent will turn their head back towards the Bench and glower at us with a look that could kill.

CHAPTER FOUR

At home, my wife Caroline and I had the house to ourselves at the time. Our son and daughter had both left home by then and lived some distance away.

Our sole companion was a beautiful Irish setter the colour of dark red wine, getting on a bit after a long life as a dearly loved member of the family. She was eleven years old, greying at the muzzle and spending her days padding around our large garden and paddock or lying stretched out in the sunshine or before the sitting-room fire, depending upon the season.

Completely useless as a guard dog, she had always welcomed visitors with a wag of her tail and loping up to them for a sniff. Even the postman was a friend.

One day that summer, as the evenings began to lengthen and May gave way to June, Caroline and I had walked up the lane to call in on a neighbour, leaving our setter Ruby to wander around the garden.

On our return twenty minutes later we went straight

indoors to deal with this and that, and to get together some lunch. It was not until a couple of hours later that Caroline said, "Where's Ruby? She must be still outside." Normally on our coming back to the house she would re-join us and flop herself down under the kitchen table.

"I'll go and enquire," I replied, leaving my cup of coffee on the Aga.

I ambled around the garden and then gave a sharp whistle or two. No sign of her. The gate into the paddock was open, so I thought she may have shambled around the hedge to the far end, where there are often interesting wildlife smells.

I followed the hedge around one side, and kept whistling and calling.

Nothing.

I walked across the pasture and did the same along the other side, back out to the white gate onto the road in the furthest corner.

Not a sign of Ruby anywhere.

The gate was shut and reasonably dog-proof, certainly for a large setter.

It was then I noticed the scrap of cardboard wedged into the hunting latch at the top of the gate. I drew it out and opened it, to reveal some words scrawled in capitals with a black marker pen: 'NOW YOULL KNOW WHAT ITS LIKE TO MISS YOR PAL.'

A cold chill ran straight down my back. Instantly the pieces of the vague jigsaw puzzle in my subconscious clicked into place. I remembered the last anonymous message stuck onto my windscreen in the Law Courts car park, the curious behaviour of Tee-Shirt at the bus stop and in the courtroom gallery, and his unidentified back view in the police inspector's warrant application.

I ran back to the house and handed the piece of card wordlessly to Caroline as I made for the telephone in the kitchen. There I paused before dialling. This was part of a saga, not a dire emergency. I pressed 101 rather than 999.

The police followed standing instructions to the letter. They are asked to prioritise calls from a member of the judiciary phoning with concerns for their personal safety, and an officer turned up in a marked car about half an hour later.

It helped that I knew him. He had until a year or so back been our Community PC for the group of villages up our end of the valley, and had been a familiar face at parish council meetings and in the local school.

Sadly those days are long gone. Government cuts have made rural community policing a mourned thing of the past.

Over a cup of coffee (mine had long since gone cold on the Aga lid), with a pale Caroline by my side, I outlined the connections I had just linked together between my sightings of Tee-Shirt and my growing conviction that these had something to do with a court case in which he had taken umbrage over the outcome, and was targeting me in order to 'get his own back'.

I was sure now that he had, creepily, been watching our house and grounds that day and had chosen his moment to snatch Ruby from the paddock and whisk her away, presumably in his silver Merc. I dug out its registration number and handed it over.

The name of the inspector who had called in earlier, and the search warrant reference number that I still held, I passed across as well.

The officer departed with the formal intention to seek a suspect for the crime of 'harassment, alarm and distress', and Caroline tried to cheer me up.

"Well, at least we already have a likely suspect," she pointed out. "Remember the poor Spencers down the road whose whippet was taken by a van driver and it was months before they heard anything? The police found her on a caravan site up north on a routine chip identification and she was brought home not much the worse for wear."

"But Ruby's so old and frail," I replied. "I do hope they treat her kindly until she's found. At least she's got a chip."

It was only then that I remembered the sighting of Tee-Shirt on the garage forecourt, with the schoolboy in the car.

The schoolboy.

My memory flashed back to that school presentation and the odd behaviour of the lad near the front of the class.

Were they one and the same? Was he Tee-Shirt's son? Was my name anathema to his entire household?

I was soon to find out.

*

What would the police do first? Presumably they would go to the home of the registered keeper of the Mercedes as the first step in looking for Ruby. They would not, I thought, need a search warrant. This was an identified criminal offence currently being committed, and immediate arrest would be anticipated. But I was not certain.

I thought then of the house and garage only ten minutes' drive from my home, where Tee-Shirt had been filmed by the detective constable. Might he have taken Ruby there?

I was worried for our old dog. Whatever I may or may not have done to offend Tee-Shirt and his family, Ruby was entirely innocent and vulnerable. Would they feed her properly? She had medication in her supper food. How long could she go on without that?

It could be some days before the police followed up my reported link between Tee-Shirt and the house on the county boundary.

It was early evening by then. Ruby's supper time. I thought long and hard with the germ of an idea that had been growing over the last few hours.

At last I said to Caroline, "It's no good, I can't sit around waiting for something to turn up. I'm going to go along to the house in Ludford myself and have a snoop around. I have a feeling that Ruby is being held there."

"James, don't be so silly," she replied. "It's far too dangerous. You might get hurt, or even worse. You might get held yourself. I should leave it to the police."

"But it may be too late. Poor Ruby. Anyway, I am being got at by these people and I don't like it.

"I'm only going to investigate. I promise I won't confront anyone. In fact I don't intend to be seen at all.

"Promise," I repeated.

Caroline looked anxious, but I gave her a hug and picked up the car keys.

CHAPTER FIVE

I was not sure quite where the house lay. Ludford was bisected by the A road beside which stood the village shop, the butcher's and the farm shop, with the large pub opposite. Steep narrow lanes ran off to north and south.

I had a hunch the house would be approached from the south, and so I took the single-track lane opposite the shop. This took me down to a valley bottom and a stream with iron railings. Up the other side was a fork in the road. I paused. From here on was best by foot.

I parked the car by the old mill pond and decided to try the left-hand fork first. This took me uphill for a quarter of a mile, where the tarmac petered out at the entrance to a farmyard. There was an old cottage, but nothing resembling the house in the body-cam recording.

I turned around and started to walk back downhill. Then, looking across the valley fields to my left, there it was, clearly accessed from the right fork off the lane where I had parked the car. I then thought, why approach the house from the road and the entrance gate? If I am snooping, better to go straight across country from here and take a look through the shrubbery at the back.

Finding a field gate, I climbed over into a pasture of long grass, rather neglected and infested with dock and thistle. Crossing that, I scrambled through a gap in the far hedge and into a similar pasture. There at the far side lay the rear fence of the garden and an overgrown shrubbery belonging to the drug dealer's house.

Unfortunately it was still very much daylight, but the sun was casting long shadows almost directly before me, so I kept low to the ground and in the lengths of tree shadow, until I reached the fence.

Clambering through the plain wire fence was easy. Now I crouched in the density of the tangled shrubs that covered at least half of the rear garden. I pushed my way carefully through the undergrowth trying to avoid snapping twigs underfoot. From the shadow of the rampant buddleia and decrepit old crab apple trees I paused and studied the rear wall of the house which now lay only about ten yards before me across a strip of abandoned lawn.

Several windows on both ground and first floors gazed out blankly across the lawn. Some had curtains, undrawn, and unsurprisingly for the time of day there were no house lights burning.

No movement or sound, except a distant tractor well out of sight away behind me to the east.

I was rather expecting the house to be unoccupied, that is to say unlived-in. If the police had made a successful bust after my search warrant approval, they would presumably have removed all evidence of drug-dealing and illicit tobacco, and arrested the man who lived there. In that event, he would undoubtedly by now be remanded in custody. My colleagues on the Bench, whoever they might have been, would scarcely have granted bail to a character found in the circumstances described to me by the officers seeking the warrant all those weeks ago.

I also found it hard to believe that a man engaged in that level of serious crime would have done so in a house containing wife and children.

Surely he had been the only resident?

*

I crept around the edge of the shrubbery until I was opposite the corner of the house. If I made a dash for the rear wall from here, visibility from a window would be much diminished by the acute angle and the depth of the window reveals.

I made the dash, and flattened myself against the wall with my back to the brickwork.

Still not a sound. I gave out a long breath. Then with new resolve I lowered myself below the nearest windowsill and very slowly raised my head to see in through the glass.

The room was completely bare except for the curtains. It had probably been the dining room in better days, its herringbone pattern woodblock floor now heavily scuffed and grubby. Dust marks showed that the room had recently been used for storing large cartons, perhaps more of that illicit cigarette contraband. Its owner, or maybe the police, had now cleared it all away, evidently.

I ducked down again and shuffled along to the next window. The curtains here had only been partially drawn back and it was hard to see in. This appeared to be one end of a large sitting room and lay in heavy shadow.

I moved on. Sure enough the French doors I came to on the right revealed the other end of the sitting room, with a fireplace and mantelpiece.

I peered around the edge of the glazing. There was a dark red carpet, bordered and patterned in faux-Persian style. In the far corner was an armchair, an ancient prickly affair with a long, deep seat in which one would have to sit almost horizontally, reminiscent of the furniture in the stuffier London clubs of St James'.

Fast asleep on the chair, her old head resting characteristically on one arm, lay Ruby.

A steel saucepan of water stood nearby, and a china plate with the remains of something presumably edible.

Otherwise, the room seemed to be empty of life.

I knelt on the ground and did some quick thinking. Surely I had been irresponsible enough already with this adventure, without adding to the risk. The sensible course now would have been to withdraw silently to the shrubbery and retrace my steps to the car and home, from where I could have telephoned the police and reported what I had seen.

Of course, the police would ultimately have given me a good ticking-off, in the most courteous terms, for interfering with their investigation and putting myself at risk.

But then again, there was our dear Ruby, virtually within arm's reach. Once through the French doors and six strides across the room, I could have hauled Ruby by the collar and within half a minute we would have squeezed through the garden fence into the field behind, and away. This picture gave me much satisfaction to contemplate. One in the eye for Tee-Shirt.

I dearly wanted to rescue Ruby. She seemed to be all right, but what if her kidnapper turned nasty – or decided to take her somewhere else?

I reached across the glass to the brass door handle and carefully turned it. Please, please don't let the doors be locked.

The door gave and I pulled it slowly ajar. There was a slight creak of a rusty hinge, then another. Ruby heard it and awoke, raising her head off the arm of the chair, and looked over towards me.

Her tail thumped on the seat cushion. I stepped gingerly over the threshold and tiptoed onto the carpet.

I was halfway across the room when the door from the hall beyond opened noisily and Tee-Shirt entered, carrying a cardboard box.

I froze. He did not see me immediately but walked over to a bookshelf and deposited his box.

I held my breath in a rather futile manner. He then noticed that Ruby's head was raised and pointing in concentration at something in the centre of the room. Me.

He followed her gaze.

CHAPTER SIX

For about four seconds we stared at each other in complete silence, both of us immobile.

I was the first to speak.

"So, it was you all along. I thought as much." I could not think what else to say. I noticed that, for a change, he was not wearing his trademark shirt but a nondescript grey jogging top.

He had recovered quickly from the initial surprise. With a sneer he came a few steps closer and bunched his right hand into a fist.

"And wotcher gonna do abaht it, then, mister clever magistrate?"

An unlikely calm came over me at this point. I realised in that fleeting moment that despite appearances I held the upper hand. Information is a powerful tool. He who holds the key information in any given situation has a keen advantage over him who does not.

"Well," I began, "perhaps you'd like to know why I

thought I might find you here, in this house. It's not your home, is it? It belongs to a friend of yours" – and here I hoped my judgement was sound – "at present in custody on a number of serious charges."

A pause.

"Dunno wot you're talking abaht. I got your dog 'ere, that's all." But he had released his fist and averted his eyes to the floor.

"You have, and I have come to take her away again. I think you should realise that my wife knows I am here, and the police are already aware that this is one of the places where they might find our kidnapped red setter.

"I dare say there are one or two other things of interest they may find here too," I added as an inspired afterthought.

Tee-Shirt's eyes slid involuntarily to the cardboard box over on the bookcase shelf.

"The police may be here any minute," I hazarded with a display of confidence that I was very far from feeling.

I pressed on. "Anyway, what I want to know is – what have you got against me? What do you think I've done that causes you to target me in the way you have? I really have no idea."

This was an unfortunate thing to say. Tee-Shirt's eyes suddenly sparked fire and again he clenched his fist and stuck out his chin aggressively. "Nah, yer don't, do yer? Yer have no idea in yer head, yer stuck-up magistrate layin' dan the law in yer posh voice an' causin' us ordinary folk a lot o' grief.

"Well, mister smart arse, let me tell you. You an' your other two so-called Wash-ups put away my boy Wayne fer twenty months the day after 'is seventeenth birfday fer

Grievous, when the Probation had only recommended a Youf Rehab Order. My boy. Me an' the missus need our Wayne, an' his young brother Danny dotes on 'im, 'ee does. So, see, I'm takin' the matter inter me own hands an' teachin' you a lesson yer'll never ferget. See?"

Now I could recall the case. It is quite rare in our court to send youths to a Young Offenders' Institution, particularly for a term close to our maximum of two years.

Wayne Bruggs. Oh yes, I remember him.

*

Some youngsters up before us for quite violent offences take us by surprise. They are small for their age, articulate and polite in the courtroom. No sign of aggression or even ebullience, and accompanied by a parent or two who give every appearance of a responsible attitude towards their children in the face of complex economic and other dire domestic circumstances.

Wayne Bruggs represented none of these characteristics. He was, frankly, a brute. Overgrown for his age, the leader of a feral gang of kids on his estate, and with a string of previous offences of assault, harassment and criminal damage, culminating in several burglaries before the severe attack on an elderly gentleman that had landed him in Portland with a Detention and Training Order.

The Youth Offending Teams had done their best throughout Wayne's criminal career to date, beginning with a ten-month Referral Order when he was only fourteen years old.

In those days he had occasionally been accompanied voluntarily by his mother at his court appearances. On other occasions she had been summoned to court up until his sixteenth birthday, following which he was always in court on his own.

His father had never put in an appearance on any occasion at all.

Once or twice during his sixteenth year, the Youth Offending Team had managed to extract from Wayne a spark of expressed interest in attending the local college for a course in bricklaying, and the Court had seized on this as a glimmer of light and hoped that at last he was beginning to take life more seriously, and might even end up in the employment of a singularly benevolent and long-suffering building contractor, if only on a casual basis.

But this was always 'pie in the sky'. We bent over backwards, as we are obliged to do, to formulate sentences which placed the present and future behaviour of Wayne Bruggs at the centre of the disposal, but he was one of those young people who are almost impervious to moral influence, let alone a personal responsibility under the law. I say 'almost' because I believe no one to be beyond redemption, but the institution of English justice is a blunt and inadequate tool to hone a youngster such as Wayne. His promotion from the Youth Court to the Adult Magistrates' Court was doomed to be seamless.

From what I had now seen and experienced of his father up to that evening confrontation in the lonely house at Ludford, Wayne's future had my dismal sympathy. With a role model like that, life would be severely handicapped.

Wayne would need an entirely new environment, new social circle and new economic circumstances if he was ever to stand a chance of recovery.

*

I had no opportunity for these reflections at the time, of course. I was face to face with an angry, heavily built man who was itching to let fly at me, and with little capacity to judge the consequences.

And he had my dog. Ruby lay on the chair behind him and there was no way I could make a grab for her collar and escape through the French doors.

My only option was to slow things down and play along with Mr Bruggs until some other course presented itself.

Behind me was a solitary old dining chair near the wall. I sat down carefully, and tried to look relaxed.

"I'm afraid I am not allowed to discuss your son Wayne's sentence," I stated firmly. "You may think that magistrates can say and do whatever they like, but that is far from true. We have to follow what Parliament has intended and what the higher courts, the senior judges, have previously determined.

"Now, how is stealing my dog or staring at me in court going to help Wayne?

"What are you going to say to the police when they get here?"

I fervently hoped they would get there very soon. This temporising dialogue with Tee-Shirt could not be extended for much longer.

"Ah won't 'ave ter say nuffink, 'cos ah won't be 'ere," he muttered. "Ah'm orf in the motor, an' you're comin wiv me, raht now."

With that, he pulled from his rear pocket a flick knife and sprung the blade, which looked extremely sharp.

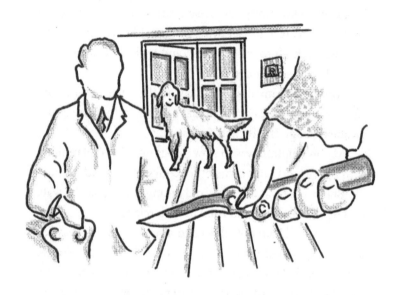

I was not going to argue but tried to play for time.

"Look," I said, "kidnapping a dog because of a grievance you have with its owner is one thing.

"Kidnapping a magistrate at knifepoint because you don't like the sentence imposed on your son is going to land you in very deep water indeed. This will be a judge in the Crown Court and several years in prison. You do realise that, don't you?"

I stayed put on my chair and waited.

CHAPTER SEVEN

Bruggs held the knife out in front of him and came up to within a yard of me. He was sweating badly, beads forming on his forehead and dark patches under the arms of his jogging top.

"We're goin' for a ride, you 'n' me, whatever you say, mister magistrate, so let's go."

He jabbed the flick knife in the air in front of my face, and I winced, involuntarily jerking my head back.

Then from the far corner of the room began a low, rumbling sound, developing into a deep growl. Bruggs spun round and I darted a glance around him over towards the old armchair.

Ruby was rising from her position and was now standing four-square on the seat cushion. Her jowls were slowly drawing back to reveal two rows of large, pointed white teeth. Sharp teeth.

I had not seen a snarl on our Ruby quite like that since the occasion years ago when a young vixen had come through the fence into our garden sniffing around for something to feed her cubs down at the bottom of the lane.

Bruggs' face was in profile to me. In that instant I knew that he was petrified. He clearly knew nothing of dogs and he had frozen rigid.

But he still held the flick knife.

Dear old Ruby. Her leg muscles were quite incapable of springing anywhere, and I doubt that her jaw muscles would have made much impression on human flesh beneath a jogging top; but she was no more conscious of her fallibilities than was Bruggs.

For a few moments there was a stand-off between the two of them. I think my presence in the room had been completely forgotten.

What precipitated the action next was again Ruby's initiative. She sat up on her haunches and began to bark. The bark of a red setter is renowned for being audible across three counties, and Ruby's lung power had not suffered the same deterioration as her physique.

She barked loudly and at length. The French doors to the sitting room were still wide open, and the sound must have ricocheted around the Ludford valley.

Soon every farm collie and stockbroker Labrador in the entire parish were enquiring urgently and at volume what all the fuss was about.

A donkey in the field adjoining the garden started braying. I guess that was the last straw for Tee-Shirt. He hesitated briefly, uncertain whether to attempt to retrieve the cardboard box from the bookcase behind Ruby's chair, but thinking better of it he gave Ruby one more scared glance and rushed through the open doorway out into the garden and around the side of the house.

Within seconds his car engine was revving and with a squeal of tyres on gravel he was gone.

Ruby substituted her bark with a low growl and plodded to the doorway. She cocked one floppy ear as though to assure herself that the menace had truly vanished, and turned to me with a pleased expression and a wildly wagging tail to push her damp muzzle onto my lap, looking up with large liquid setter eyes that said all too plainly, "Didn't I do well?"

*

Magistrates these days are encouraged to hold police presence in court at the same degree of impartial arm's length as representatives of any other agency appearing before us. This was not always the case.

A good many years ago now, summary prosecutions in the Magistrates' Courts were conducted by police officers in uniform. The proceedings themselves were known as the Police Courts. In those days it was widely assumed that the Justices on the Bench and the police officers conducting the case were all on the same side.

Now, of course, prosecutions are led in court by a solicitor or barrister employed by the Crown Prosecution Service (or a lawyer engaged by the CPS as agent). The police presenting a charge need to satisfy the independent CPS that the evidence in the charge meets two criteria: that it demonstrates a reasonable chance of conviction, and that a prosecution is in the public interest. The bar for both of these criteria is often regarded by the police as unnecessarily high, and can lead to controversy and discontent.

The police presence in a court case is confined now to the role of witness, and the police officers concerned must present their evidence orally to the same standard as any other witness. (There are some exceptions laid down as precedent from the higher courts, such as the presumption that, in the absence of evidence to the contrary, roadside speed cameras are functioning accurately.)

Police officers are, as a result, occasionally rebuked by the Bench for inadequate preparation or presentation of evidence in the witness box. One or two of the more severe Presiding Justices might also pass adverse comment on an officer witness' standard of dress in court.

Naturally enough, the 'quid pro quo' applies outside the court. A magistrate stopped by the police on the road for breaking the law, a suspected drink/drive offence, for example, or indeed for any purpose for which the police are seeking help or cooperation, is treated by the officer no differently than any other person, even if they are recognised.

If a JP is stopped by the police for any kind of infringement, the casual mention of one's magisterial role would be a serious mistake, almost certain to have precisely the opposite effect to that which one was misguided enough to assume.

Generally speaking, however, I would hazard that magistrates – in or out of court – are unaccustomed to being rebuked by police officers.

Such, nevertheless, was inevitably to be my own experience following the adventure in Ludford that evening on my return home with Ruby.

*

My exploits had seemed to me to be a long-drawn-out affair, and I was anxious that Caroline would have been so worried about my prolonged absence that she would have telephoned the police to search for me.

On my arrival home, however, she was busy in the kitchen preparing supper and no more relieved to see me than was to be expected after the madcap scheme I had determined upon. Her main reaction was the joy at being reunited with Ruby and her congratulations on my rescue.

Caroline's response rapidly cooled, however, as I sat down with a much-needed stiff whisky and gave her the unexpurgated report of my confrontation with Tee-Shirt.

"You are a total idiot, James," she said. "What are the police going to say to you now? Taking the law into your own hands, putting yourself in danger and unnecessarily risking the expensive resources of the emergency services if it had all gone horribly wrong."

I sighed and had to admit that her crisp summary of the position was unlikely to be bettered by anything said to me by the police when I phoned them to report.

This I proceeded to do without delay. I was fortunate in being able to speak to the officer in charge of the case, whom I had known from his local Community Officer days.

He became very stern and told me to remain where I was

as he would drive out, take a statement from me and carry on to Ludford to inspect the scene of my adventure for himself.

I draw a veil over the dressing-down he delivered, in a most courteous manner, on his arrival half an hour later. This was quite definitely a 'meeting without coffee'.

I signed a formal and quite detailed statement, in which I noted carefully that the French doors at the house were unlocked, so that I could not be accused of breaking and entering.

I had of course been trespassing, but that is of no interest to the police. That would be a civil infringement for which the only penalty could be a County Court fine on finding that I had caused the owner of the property demonstrable and measurable damage.

Any other potential offence I was confident of evading, as I was searching what I believed to be an unoccupied building for property of my own, viz. one dog which I had good reason to believe was in danger to life and limb.

Even so, my conversation with the officer was educationally humiliating – rather constructively so, I thought afterwards. Now, as a magistrate I had personal experience of the routine imposed on witnesses and other parties appearing before me on the wrong side of the bench. Not a comfortable experience.

My self-esteem was slightly restored as the officer was about to take his leave. I remembered to suggest to him that he take a close look inside the cardboard box on the shelf in the Ludford sitting room, as this might be a further avenue to explore with Tee-Shirt when he and his colleagues finally caught up with him.

CHAPTER EIGHT

Unlike the Family Court, which has a fair amount of documentation to read through before a day's sitting (though not the reams of paperwork needed days in advance, as used to be the case before an enlightened senior judge simplified the system), the Magistrates' Court and Youth Court begin a day's sitting with no prior information on the cases before them.

The court listing, preferably on paper but increasingly just on a screen, is handed to the magistrates in the retiring room just before the court convenes at ten o'clock.

In the days when legal and administrative court staff were plentiful, the case list would be on our table when we arrived at 9:15. The legal adviser, then called the Clerk to the Justices, would join us at 9:30 and give an analysis of each case, highlighting the unusual or difficult elements, and helpfully giving us the Sentencing Guidelines' page number for each of the offences listed.

Sadly, no more. The acute understaffing these days

mean that the case list is handed out at about 9:45, and the legal adviser rushes in at five minutes to ten for a fleeting resumé of one or two cases, before we process into court and get underway.

Some of us still insist on commencing at ten o'clock even when we know quite well that none of the cases are ready to appear before us. Some vestige of judicial administrative authority and self-discipline still remains.

One feature of the routine of summary justice has always existed, however. The magistrates rota'd to sit on any particular day have no advance notice of the names of the offenders or dependants who will be standing before us during the course of the sitting.

This means that if, after a cursory glance at the list in the retiring room, the name of a person is revealed with whom I am too well acquainted in other spheres, I would have to 'sit back' from that case. Occasionally, it is not until that person enters the courtroom and is recognised by a magistrate that 'sitting back' must be volunteered.

A similar issue can apply with witnesses at a trial. In that case, recognition will only occur as the witness is called, or is recognised in the witness box.

In any of these cases of acquaintance recognition, the magistrate concerned is in an awkward position. He or she cannot simply excuse themselves and withdraw to the retiring room for yet another cup of instant brew. No, they are obliged to 'sit back' in the courtroom itself, or down in an empty seat in the public gallery. The reason for this rule is to be able to demonstrate to all parties that, when the two remaining justices have retired to decide verdict or sentence, they are not being privately influenced by the magistrate who has 'sat back'.

All well and good, but such occasions can be acutely embarrassing to both the defendant and the magisterial friend, colleague or close relative. Their relationship thereafter can be difficult to resume unaffected.

In the case of witnesses at a trial, experienced magistrates will take care to notice any clue in the case listing, such as an address, or from the legal adviser's briefing. If one has a sixth sense, it is wise to obtain the witnesses' names before the trial begins. Recognising a name and 'sitting back' or withdrawing at that stage of the day can avoid much difficulty. Sometimes, if appropriate, all the witnesses can be asked to enter the public gallery before the trial commences, so that the magistrates can see whether there are faces 'too close to home' that they recognise.

The decision to 'sit back' or 'recuse' is that of the magistrate alone. Only he or she can make a judgement as to whether the acquaintance in the courtroom is sufficiently close to run the risk of personal bias – or equally importantly, to risk an accusation of bias by one or other of the parties concerned in the case.

Of course, even in today's amalgamated courts, covering a huge geographical catchment area (in my case an entire county), individual repeat offenders will become very familiar to the magistracy. If they are there for sentencing, such familiarity is unimportant because their previous convictions will be part of the documentation to be considered when imposing a sentence.

In the case of a trial, however, the presence of an 'old lag' in the dock and pleading 'not guilty' needs great care. No assumptions can be made. Magistrates are trained, and expected, to cast from their minds all remembrance of past behaviour (unless 'bad character' has been adduced beforehand by the parties to be declared at the hearing).

Sometimes, in similar vein, information may be given by a witness at a trial which is inadmissible (such as a defendant's involvement in another offence linked to the matter at the trial). Again, magistrates must dismiss from their minds what they have heard.

This is naturally difficult to do, and requires a conscious commitment by all three Justices hearing the trial, and an acknowledgment in open court accordingly.

The great and majestic principle of the law of England, sadly unknown in so many foreign legislatures, is paramount: a defendant is not obliged to prove anything. The burden of proof rests solely with the prosecution. Every defendant is innocent unless or until proved guilty – and all such proof is confined strictly to the oral and written evidence presented at the trial in the courtroom.

It is for this reason that 'justice' can never be equated to 'truth'. If a case for the prosecution or for the defence is handled badly by those presenting evidence in the courtroom, justice will be served by the Bench according to the quality of that evidence and it may well fail to have represented the truth of the matter.

Magistrates dispense justice within the laws of the land. We can never claim to have established the truth in any absolute sense.

*

And so it was that one day a few months after my adventure with Ruby, my two colleagues and I were in the retiring room preparing to hear the three trials listed for our all-day sitting.

Our legal adviser had been dealing with a tricky last-minute procedural issue with one of the defending advocates, and was only able to give us five minutes' briefing before we entered the courtroom at ten o'clock.

The first trial listed was for a car theft, known as 'taking a vehicle without the owner's consent' (known in the trade as a TWOC), in the name of no one I knew, although it rang a distant bell from somewhere in my memory. He appeared in the dock having been brought in a prison van from Reading, as he was in custody on remand, possibly for another offence, of which of course we were told nothing.

The prosecutor set out the facts of the case, prior to calling his first witness. The car alleged to have been stolen had been used for transporting illicit imports, and had been seized by the police at an address in the village of Ludford, an isolated property on the border with the adjacent county.

Suddenly, I remembered where I had heard the name of the defendant before. He had been the owner or occupier of the house for which, all those months previously, I had granted a search warrant for drug-trafficking and illegal cigarette importation.

That had also been the premises, of course, where Ruby had been kidnapped and where I had experienced the altercation with Bruggs.

Now, neither of those incidents had any relevance to the case of car theft before us.

Maybe the defendant was on remand for the drug-dealing and illicit importation issue, but that was surmise on my part, and of no consequence to the question of car theft.

The fact that it was I who had granted that search warrant was perhaps something I should declare in open court, but it was unlikely that the defending advocate would have objected to my sitting on this present case, which was based on evidence of a car stolen from a garage forecourt in Bournemouth.

In light of all that had gone before, should I disqualify myself from sitting on this trial? Would my personal experiences with Tee-Shirt, a man I had good reason to believe to be an associate of the person in the dock before me, risk prejudicing my contribution to a verdict decision?

When in due course I would appear in court myself as a prosecution witness in the harassment by Tee-Shirt (unless he pleaded guilty), and the facts and motives in that story were all exposed in open court, would that be grounds for a legal challenge against a 'guilty' verdict in the present case on the premise that I was likely to have been biased?

Would my long experience and training as a Justice of the Peace in 'dismissing from my mind' such peripheral information both avoid bias and be accepted by all concerned to have done so?

CHAPTER NINE

To have disqualified myself from sitting on the day of the trial would create procedural and judicial difficulties.

Neither of my two colleagues were Presiding Justices, but the trial could go ahead with just two magistrates if one of them had bravely agreed to take the chair on this one occasion.

A preferable solution would be to bring in another Presiding Justice who might happen to be in the court building, or summoned quickly from home if living nearby. Neither would be likely.

Alternatively, the trial could be adjourned to another day, at huge inconvenience to witnesses and others. It would also mean delay, probably for at least a month.

"Justice delayed is justice denied."

*

In the event, my dilemma was resolved quite decisively.

I stopped the proceedings, which had scarcely got beyond the prosecutor's opening introduction, and in a moment of inspiration asked for a list of all witnesses' names.

Among the prosecution witnesses was a certain A Bruggs. So, Tee-Shirt had decided to cooperate with the police, had he? Well, that made it easy for me. I could not possibly preside over a trial at which Tee-Shirt was to be a material witness.

I stood down, and my colleagues continued the hearing. This meant that I had to 'sit back', and so joined the motley onlookers in the public gallery.

That was not the end of my conundrum. Tee-Shirt, whom I now knew to be Andy Bruggs, duly gave his evidence against his former associate, stating that he had himself been in Bournemouth and had watched the man talking to another and being handed the keys of the car alleged to have been stolen off the forecourt, having tried (he said) to persuade him not to do so.

Bruggs was thanked by the Bench for giving his evidence, and invited either to leave the court – with strict instruction not to talk to anyone outside about the case at least until it was concluded – or, if he wished, to sit in the public gallery to hear the remainder of the trial.

He opted for the latter.

Entirely unaware of my presence at the back of the courtroom, he sauntered from the witness box and plonked himself down heavily in a seat alongside my own, his attention fully given to the sour expression on the face of his former colleague in the dock.

Here we then were, in an absurd situation. Side by side were a dog-kidnapping harasser facing an additional charge of threatening behaviour with a knife, and alongside, his victim on each of these offences; both sitting in a Magistrates' Court and one of us a Justice of the Peace.

What was I to do? The vital thing was to avoid any disruption or distraction to the proceedings, which had now moved on to the appearance and oath-taking of a second witness for the prosecution.

I turned my head aside from my close companion and thought hard. Ideally I should slip away quietly before he noticed me. But if I left the courtroom, might my absence be seen to prejudice the impartiality of the trial Bench, or at least be an excuse for the defending advocate to express doubts?

"Justice must not only be done but be seen to be done."

There were no other public seats available for me to shift position.

I could write a brief note on a page torn from my diary, for the usher to hand up to the legal adviser, saying that I had to leave the courtroom but would not return to the retiring room. She could then pass the note to both advocates. That would do it. Everyone would be happy.

On the other hand, fiddling about with my diary and pen and then catching the eye of the usher to pass it over, was bound to attract the attention of Bruggs. What exactly would happen if he recognised who it was sitting close by him?

I was soon to discover.

*

The prosecution on that occasion was being led by a young man at the early stage of his career with the Crown Prosecution Service. He was a solicitor but, from the manner in which he conducted himself, clearly intended one day to be a famous barrister.

I could see that he was a relative novice, because I recognised a familiar court prosecutor of long standing seated alongside him and occasionally responding to his colleague with a whispered piece of advice.

Nonetheless, the poor chap was not doing very well. For one thing, he had been sitting in one too many Crown Court trials with judge and jury. In that court, the advocates for both prosecution and defence need to play to the jury with all the dramatic powers of persuasion they can muster, knowing that they are addressing lay folk from a wide variety of backgrounds with no prior experience or training in the interpretation of evidence; and most of whom will never have been in a courtroom before.

Magistrates, on the other hand, do not take kindly to this style of role-playing advocacy, which is often presented in a rather condescending manner. Many of us will have been weighing difficult court evidence ever since this particular prosecutor was just out of nappies.

This was, sadly, not his only error. His examination-in-chief of his witnesses, including Bruggs, had centred on a great deal of factual information, but he had severely neglected two fundamental principles.

Firstly, he needed to identify, and then satisfy, all of the statutory elements of the offence. Every criminal offence, in law, has one or more defined elements that all have to be proved in order to secure conviction.

Most (but not all) require the basic proof of 'intent' – that the action was actually intended rather than being purely accidental. Some offences can be proved without 'intent', instead being committed 'recklessly'. An action which was reasonably avoidable in the circumstances of the case could be construed as criminal recklessness, for example criminal damage.

The case before the Court that day was the 'taking' of a vehicle. If this was a temporary intention (for example as a getaway car after a crime, that would then be abandoned or returned) it could not be a 'theft', because theft has a rather tricky offence element – it requires the intention 'permanently to deprive'.

The word 'permanently' has a long and colourful history of interpretation and application in the arsenal of tactics by advocates for the defence.

The details of this case play no part in my story, but suffice it to say that the prosecutor lamentably omitted to fulfil his obligation in this respect: not just one or two, but every statutory element of an offence needs to be proved in order to secure conviction. If just one element is omitted, or gives rise to a reasonable doubt, the prosecution fails.

The second fundamental principle that he failed to recognise that day was the role of the defence advocate, who took her turn after the prosecution case was completed. She needed to prove nothing. Her job was to undermine the case that we had just heard, including the pulling apart of the evidence given by the prosecution witnesses by rigorous cross-examination. Whatever the elements of the offence, her responsibility was to sow seeds of doubt in the minds of the Bench. Her objective was clear-cut: if the prosecution case was not proved 'beyond reasonable doubt', she had won.

The trial duly ran its course, and the two magistrates retired to determine their verdict. Sitting there on tenterhooks at the back, I just hoped that they would be of one mind, otherwise we were all set for a long evening.

CHAPTER TEN

A quarter of an hour elapsed as we waited, during which I sat sideways away from Bruggs with my hand supporting my chin and shielding my face, while he stayed immobile, ignoring all around him.

The legal adviser was called out to the retiring room to give advice requested by the Bench. Great care is needed then, in order to avoid false impressions. Professional advice on the law and on procedure may be given, but under no circumstances can the legal adviser offer opinion on verdict.

Most advisers then return to the courtroom and inform the parties of the nature of the advice given. Justice must be seen to be open and not secret.

After another ten minutes one of the occupants of a public seat behind me became bored, and got up to leave.

I quietly and surreptitiously slid out of my chair and around into the rear seat. Here I breathed more easily and contemplated the back of Bruggs' shaved head. Even from that angle I could see he was looking worried and was beginning to sweat.

It occurred to me that ever since 'turning King's evidence' he had assumed that the defendant would be found guilty of the TWOC and that, aggravated by his list of previous convictions (most of which were familiar to Bruggs), he would be sent into immediate custody.

I could almost see the cogs slowly turning in Bruggs' brain. He was beginning to ask himself a new question – what if the defendant was released? Where would that put Bruggs?

I read 'revenge' and 'retribution' writ large on his furrowed brow.

The defendant was in the dock on remand in custody. But what for? Perhaps it was for this alleged offence alone, in which case Bruggs had good reason to be nervous.

*

The two magistrates returned to the courtroom. The lady in the chair cleared her throat and opened her notes and the verdict form.

Both the defendant and Bruggs stared intently at the floor.

"The Court is not satisfied that the prosecution has proved all elements of this offence beyond reasonable doubt," began the pronouncement. Several reasons were given, all to the obvious chagrin of the inexperienced prosecutor.

"We therefore find you not guilty of this offence. Take a seat, please.

"Does the defence wish to make an application?" A discussion and agreement followed in relation to costs.

"Very well, you are free to go."

I folded my arms and smiled to myself. This could be interesting. A spectator at the Roman Games, about to watch a one-time gladiator being confronted by a wounded lion. If the gladiator had any sense he would make it to the door first.

Unfortunately, the usher had moved to the door of the dock to unlock it, and the security officer from the public hallway had chosen that moment to enter the courtroom, the two of them almost colliding in the corner by the entrance.

Bruggs did not stand a chance. As he dodged from one to the other looking for a gap in which to escape, the dock door swung open and the defendant, now with no further stain on his character, strode out. Pushing past his solicitor, who had also joined the hiatus at the doorway in order to shake his hand and receive some modicum of gratitude, he barged through them all and confronted Bruggs inches from his nose.

As the officer put out a restraining hand on the man's elbow, Bruggs went rapidly into reverse, backing away into the row of public seats in which I sat viewing the spectacle with several other bemused onlookers.

Then Bruggs turned, and our eyes met, only feet apart. He did a double-take and blanched visibly. His face instantly suffused into purple anger. Forgetting where he was and mindless of the consequences he grabbed me by the collar, hauled me to my feet and wrenched me around as if to set up a barricade between him and the released defendant.

By this time, the legal adviser away at the other end of the courtroom had registered the developing fracas and pressed the red button beneath his desk.

Two more officers, with handcuffs, promptly entered the room, joined by the two others who had accompanied the defendant into the dock.

The back of the courtroom was now becoming rather crowded.

Out of the corner of my eye I noticed my two colleagues on the bench prudently slipping out towards the retiring room, their role now a little superfluous.

The shouting match began. Bruggs and his erstwhile colleague began to exchange a rich and comprehensive dialogue with ever-increasing fury, drawing colourful attention to one another's parental relationships, sexual proclivities, and concepts of loyalty and fraternity; the one restrained by the grip of two security officers, the other by a burly Witness Support volunteer who had happened to be sitting next to me and who now held on to Bruggs's shoulder at his back.

Just as the two protagonists were beginning to run out of unused vocabulary and the boiling had reduced to a deep simmer, with me still standing there as piggy-in-the-middle, the cast of this little drama became augmented by the arrival – at last – of three police constables in uniform, who quickly took control and ushered both men out of the courtroom.

Peace was restored. I adjusted my collar and tie, and wandered back to the front of the court and out into the retiring room to be greeted by my colleagues with a mixture of concern and amusement, together with a welcome cup of instant brown liquid as graciously supplied by His Majesty, or at any rate His Courts & Tribunals Service.

The rest of the day, as I recollect, was fairly uneventful. I resumed the chair, and at an appropriate moment commended the Witness Support volunteer for the timely and literal manner in which he had interpreted his job description.

As we were having the usual fleeting debrief with the legal adviser at the end of the day, the office manager looked in at the retiring room and told me that a police officer was downstairs wishing to talk to me about the incident that morning.

We convened in one of the interview rooms, and I was able to explain all the circumstances from which Andy Bruggs had been prompted to react when he recognised me in the public gallery. I referred him to the case in which I was involved as a victim in the 'kidnapping' of our dog, a harassment case that was ongoing and had yet to reach first hearing in court.

The constable was one of those who had attended the incident that morning and had witnessed Bruggs holding me by the collar as a shield against his potential aggressor.

Would I wish to support a criminal charge of Assault by Beating, or alternatively one of the offences of threatening behaviour under the Public Order Act 1986?

I had already given this some thought during our lunch break. If Bruggs was charged, the case would probably be heard in tandem with the dog incident and the threatening behaviour – with a knife – in the house at Ludford. The two incidents were clearly connected.

If he pleaded guilty to both incidents, or was found so at trial, then I reckoned that the sentence for the knife crime and dog-kidnap harassment would be the substantive one, and that the assault or harassment in the courtroom that morning would merely be taken into account as an aggravating factor adding to the element of harm in the assessment of seriousness for the eventual penalty.

Depending perhaps on his previous convictions, if any, I thought it likely that his actions had passed the custody threshold well before that morning's misbehaviour.

Was there not a more constructive alternative to prosecuting the second offence?

CHAPTER ELEVEN

For several years I had been interested, along with some but not all of my colleagues, in the practice of Restorative Justice.

This was an initiative promoted by the Magistrates Association and taken up with varying enthusiasm by a number of county police constabularies.

In my county the Chief Constable and the Police and Crime Commissioner took it seriously, and I was one of the three magistrates on their Restorative Justice Scrutiny Panel which reviewed the effectiveness of its application and monitored its use as an alternative to criminal prosecution.

The idea is that, where all parties are willing, the victim and the offender communicate directly with one another to discuss and understand the harm that has been caused and the ways in which both the harm and the motivation to cause harm can be repaired.

A police officer can offer this option, at his or her discretion, as the condition to a caution or as a Community

Resolution, depending on the age of the offender. Either way it avoids a criminal charge leading to a prosecution.

That, at any rate, is the concept. In practice the outcome rarely involves a face-to-face meeting between offender and victim. Agreement to this takes a degree of courage by both parties that is seldom reached. Where it happens, the resolution can be transforming for all concerned.

Usually, however, the process involves a lesser act of reparation such as written correspondence and compensation, and its impact is diminished. Even so, reduction in rates of re-offending is encouraging.

Now, might this appeal to Andy Bruggs in response to his behaviour in court that morning?

I recalled our rather one-sided conversation in the living room of the house in Ludford. The prospects were not encouraging. But it was worth a try.

I put the case to the police officer and we went our separate ways.

*

"Had an interesting day in court?" asked Caroline over a steaming saucepan on the stove as I closed the front door and shook the raindrops off my hat.

"Pretty routine, dear, thanks. Well, apart from a minor assault."

"Oh yes? Was that a particularly difficult case then?" she responded. "I thought you got lots of those all the time."

"Um, we do, we do; though generally not inflicted on us personally. Any tea in the pot?"

A silence from the kitchen. Then Caroline appeared in the doorway.

"Gracious me, you surely didn't come to blows in the retiring room? Who on earth were you sitting with?"

I sat down at the table and related the events of the day.

*

The police had a difficult decision to take over my offer of a Restorative Justice solution to the incident in the courtroom.

Would it be appropriate to offer Andy Bruggs a Community Resolution involving remorse, preferably face to face with me, before the court dealt with the harassment and threatening behaviour at Ludford in which I was also the victim?

Eventually, the inspector handling the case agreed to this provided that Bruggs had pleaded guilty to the Ludford offences, without of course being informed that this was the condition.

At first hearing of the Ludford offences, he did choose to plead guilty, and the case was adjourned for a pre-sentence report by Probation, with a sentencing date fixed three weeks ahead.

He was granted bail, with a condition that he did not contact me in any unofficial form.

The magistracy had recently been encouraged by senior judges to consider an alternative approach, which would have been to convene a hearing of the case and to 'defer sentence' to allow a Restorative Justice session between offender and victim to take place first. A promising outcome in terms of remorse and victim awareness could then have served as a significant mitigation when the crimes were sentenced, resulting in a lesser sentence and a reduction in the likelihood of re-offending.

However, for decades the magistracy had been urged on all sides to speed up the justice process. The old practice of adjourning cases 'sine die', i.e. without fixing the earliest possible new hearing date, had long been abolished. So many of those adjournments in the old days had been on fairly spurious and unquestioned grounds.

Turnover of cases and general improvements in case management efficiency had certainly increased significantly, and deferral of cases for out-of-court negotiation or consultation had been frowned upon.

It will take several years to convince magistrates that they are encouraged to postpone the court process by allowing the parties to avoid or mitigate a criminal record by reconciliation or arbitration, but if that proves to diminish the re-offending rates it will be worthwhile. Those rates are unacceptably high at present, notoriously after a prison sentence but bad enough after community orders with probation programmes.

*

And so, the day arrived when I was to meet Andy Bruggs face to face in a charmless Probation Service office, chaperoned by a convenor drawn from the Restorative Justice team.

This meeting followed a couple of conversations

between the convenor and me to identify the issues and preferred outcomes of the proposed meeting. She had a similar conversation with Andy to explain the opportunity he now had to recognise and respond to my position as his victim, but also to describe his own motivation that induced him to behave as he did. This latter consideration is an important part of the process.

Andy was scheduled to arrive first and have an initial chat with the convenor to help set up a calm atmosphere and to assure him that neither she nor I would be confrontational. The objective was to encourage each party to understand the other's point of view.

Moving from understanding to acceptance, of course, would be different matter.

CHAPTER TWELVE

Andy and the convenor were sitting in comfortable chairs as I came in, the chairs arranged in a spaced circle of three, with a low circular table in the centre containing a water bottle, glasses and a plate of biscuits.

The convenor stood up and shook hands with me. I hesitated for a fraction of a second and then stuck out my hand to Andy, who had remained slouched in his seat. He stared resolutely at the plate of plain digestives without moving a muscle, but I kept my arm outstretched. The convenor took his seat.

Progress! At last Andy raised his eyes to meet my gesture, paused and slowly responded with a rather peremptory handshake.

The convenor and I had earlier agreed to give Andy Bruggs the floor first, to say whatever he wanted to say – within limits.

He was an unintelligent man but understood the purpose of the meeting, and no doubt had already worked out that a satisfactory outcome could well affect the sentence for the knife threat and dog-kidnap harassment to his benefit.

He was also a man with a very keen sense of loyalty to his kith and kin, placing family 'honour' well above most other moral attributes. Life had been harsh from his earliest childhood. Circumstances had built within him a bunker mentality, a defensive citadel against all comers. His wife Maureen had been 'the girl next door', that is to say in the high-rise flat next to the one rented from the council by his parents. The flats had minute balconies (all facing north), which were laden with washing lines, discarded baby buggies and fag ends. Maureen had been a buxom lass with a ready smile, a smile which had diminished steadily over their years of marriage and was now long forgotten.

Andy's pride and joy were his two sons, Wayne and Danny, the source of the few remaining shreds of affection between husband and wife.

Danny, the younger brother, was a bright lad doing well at school and the light of his mother's life. Andy imagined him one day achieving the heights of success, maybe even running his own licensed bar and club, and driving a brand-new Lexus SUV.

In Wayne, Andy recognised himself, a chip off the old block and much like his grandfather too. Wayne was the continuation of the familial bloodline. He was the totem, the ship's figurehead, the trademark Bruggs, and in that capacity could do no wrong.

All this family background I had gathered from various sources before our Restorative Justice meeting; some, perhaps, that I had obtained from my privileged

---

connections within the local justice system. I cannot deny the advantage thus gained over the limited briefing available to Andy Bruggs, one advantage amongst countless others when our respective circumstances are compared.

*

"Wull, mister," Andy began, "I is sorry abaht wot 'appened in that Law Court. Ah guess you was just in the wrong place at the wrong time." (This phrase I imagined had been supplied for him by the RJ convenor.)

"When that sod were let out o' the dock, I knew he would go for me an' I took 'old of the nearest bloke as a barrier, like, an' it 'appened to be you.

"Then when I rekernised yer as the bloke what put Wayne away an' we'd 'ad that ding-dong over yer dog, ah just saw red, ah did, an' that's just t'honest truth.

"I were only thinkin' of standin' up ter that sod when 'ee went fer me in the court; I weren't goin' fer you particler."

He paused. He had not looked up from the floor once during this speech but now gave the convenor a quick glance, as if to say, 'Is that enough?'

I was quite impressed. I felt that what he had said summed up the situation quite accurately.

The convenor poured a glass of water and placed it in front of Andy, then looked up at me brightly and gestured to me to respond.

I began by explaining why I was sitting at the back of the court in the first place. It would not be right, I said, to have taken part in the trial of his former colleague: "Because you,

Andy Bruggs, might have thought that I would be strongly biased against you as a witness. It was only fair to you, and to the man in the dock, to demonstrate that no such bias was now possible."

At this, Andy looked up into my face for the first time.

"Mr Bruggs," I continued, "I entirely accept what you have said this afternoon, and I accept your apology.

"The one thing you have not mentioned, and which naturally alarmed me at the time, is that you seized me by the collar and dragged me out of my chair with some force. That was a very uncomfortable experience and my shirt button was ripped off. Technically that was a criminal offence called 'Assault by Beating', which could have you in the dock as well as the other matters of which I was victim at your hands."

Another pause.

"I is sorry if I scared yer," came the mumbled response.

An inspired thought came to me at that moment.

"I am nearly seventy years old," I said. "Not exactly elderly, perhaps, but not as fit as I used to be."

I allowed that to sink in before proceeding. I then changed the subject completely, causing the convenor to glance at me questioningly.

"You're proud of your sons, aren't you, Mr Bruggs?" I carried on. "I remember you telling me back in that house with my dog, how much your son Wayne means to you, and how angry you were that he was sent to Portland on a Youth Detention and Training Order."

Andy reacted instantly. "Yeah, and that's why I had it in for you, 'cos you an' your lot sent 'im there."

"That's right, and do you remember what we sent him there for? Wasn't he coming out of a club in Milford Street with a crowd of drinking pals and he started pushing around an elderly gentleman standing in the bus queue, hit him and then kicked him in the back when the old man had fallen onto the pavement, bumping his head on the concrete kerb?

"He was seventy years old, too, Mr Bruggs.

"By the way, I had a very bruised shin after you dragged me across those metal seats at the back of that courtroom."

CHAPTER THIRTEEN

There was a long silence. Andy sat there with his hands on his knees, staring at the plate of biscuits. I don't think he was particularly hungry.

The convenor surreptitiously looked at his wristwatch.

"Gentlemen," he said quietly, "we ought probably to think about calling it a day. I hope this has been a helpful discussion for both of you.

"Is there anything else that either of you would like to say before we bring this session to an end?

"I will be writing up a full note of what has been said, and will send both of you a copy. If you have any points you need to raise on that, please let me know.

"Mr Bruggs, please feel free to pass a copy to your defence solicitor, as it may be in your interests to do so in relation to the hearing that you are facing."

"Thank you," I replied. "No, I have nothing further to add except to say that I am grateful to Mr Bruggs for agreeing to meet me here and discuss things."

We all stood up. Andy said nothing, but just as we were turning to the door he rubbed his right hand against his trouser leg and thrust it out towards me. I took as a token worth a thousand words.

*

This might have been expected to bring to an end all connection between the Bruggses and ourselves. I returned home to Caroline and Ruby, and our regular ordinary lives resumed once more.

I had just four months to go as a sitting magistrate. I would then reach seventy and be instantly cast into the wilderness. I would remain a Justice of the Peace for the rest of my life, as a name on the 'supplementary list'. This rather gives the impression of a kind of backup service, to be called upon to carry out certain duties of a less onerous nature. Sadly not. For the over-seventies it was a meaningless designation. I say 'was', because later the working life of judges and magistrates was extended to the age of seventy-five, too late for me to benefit.

Not that I would have chosen to do so. The magistracy was desperate for numbers, but I had felt that Parliament had taken the easy option. Far better would have been legislation that enabled the younger generations, especially the thirties and forties, to volunteer as magistrates. For that to happen, employers would have to be obliged in law to release members of staff for that purpose, perhaps under some form of financial incentive scheme. A very hard nut to crack on a national scale, and governments were not prepared to risk it.

On my seventieth birthday, my personal account on the 'eJudiciary' website would instantly be deleted, cutting me off from all the secure official communication with colleagues, His Majesty's Courts & Tribunals Service, the Ministry of Justice, the senior judiciary's news and views, the online training programmes, the daily rota appeals, and all the other paraphernalia of the Law's officialdom.

The introduction and development of this eJudiciary website, introduced when paper documents posted to our home or court addresses were abandoned, had in my experience been a very mixed blessing.

The automated rota system was brilliant, providing an easy means of notifying our non-availability for sitting dates on a six-monthly basis, and providing instant alternatives for unavoidable cancellation at short notice. Our rota coordinator, a lady of great patience, was a joy. As well as allocating last-minute changes and producing the mind-numbingly complex six-monthly allocations, we also had her personal news and views on the domestic front, accompanied by a gallery of 'smiley-face' or 'teary-face' emojis, depending on mood. A welcome human voice.

However, access to my account on eJudiciary became an increasing nightmare. The system, like every other government IT system, was designed by urban experts for use in urban areas. The characteristics of a rural environment were clearly an alien concept.

Initially, the problem was just the usual one of painfully slow download speeds on the home computer. Some email attachments opened; some did not.

What really caused the angst came later with someone's

bright idea that access to the account needed a password that had to be changed every three months, and which had to be 'verified' on opening, by means of a text or phone call from some central digital voice via a mobile phone.

In common with many other rural magistrates, I had no mobile reception of any kind at home. They tried transferring this MFA (Multi-Factor Authentication) facility to our landline. No, their digital system was not programmed for BT landlines.

A kind senior magistrate in the National Digital department then persuaded HMCTS to grant me an MFA exemption. Oh joy. That was closely followed by a senior judge's direction that MFA exemptions should be stamped out.

There then followed one of those computer sagas that, I suppose, have become so commonplace in modern life that we have come to regard them as natural and normal.

The objective reality, in truth, is that the civic discourse of official human relationships has so disintegrated, degraded, into a senseless nadir of complex mechanistic ritual that 'effectiveness' is now measured by the quantity of keyboard and screen functions to be processed, regardless of the time taken, in order to achieve an objective that in the days of paper records would have been the work of seconds.

What has emerged is a paralysis of intelligent purpose. The civic mind has warped into a state of frozen acceptance that 'series functionality' has now become the end, rather than the means to an end.

Those of us who, mercifully, still possess brains and

subjectivity that work on what might (in modern parlance) be classified an 'analogue' basis, stand back from this ludicrous state of affairs and gaze at it with objective disbelief.

I digress. This diatribe is generated (amongst other similar experiences) by the 'solution' which eventually transpired for my problem of gaining access to my eJudiciary account via MFA.

I sent an ultimatum to the Magistrates' Leadership Executive in London. Either they provided me with a practical access to my account or I would be obliged to resign instantly.

The response was fast. A girl of endless patience and courtesy from the National Digital Support Team telephoned and talked me step by step through the most tortuous series of baffling computer functions on my laptop, translating into lay English as she went along.

The objective was to set up an independent facility to enter a code number whenever I wanted to access my account. The code number would change every twenty-six seconds.

That telephone call lasted for one hour and forty-eight minutes.

My hands were shaking as I hung up. I had to go for a bit of a walk with the dog.

This is but one example of the paranoid obsession with cyber-security that afflicts our judicial bureaucracy these days.

English justice has been renowned for its public access in so many respects. Official sentencing guidelines for every individual offence; trials and sentencing of adults;

reasoned pronouncements from lowly magistrates as from Supreme Court judges; Appeal Court decisions that amend the interpretation of parliamentary legislation; all these and more are readily open to the public arena.

Obviously there are certain features of a case-in-progress that have to remain confidential – in particular those concerning young people, and civil domestic dispute; but quite honestly, what email communication to magistrates would ever be worth hacking?

CHAPTER FOURTEEN

Back to the story.

Andy Bruggs was duly committed to the Crown Court for sentencing in the Ludford case of harassment, alarm and distress, and threatening behaviour aggravated by use of a bladed article.

All things considered, the case sailed well past the custody threshold. The judge took a very dim view of the fact that the victim was not only a judicial 'colleague' but was targeted as a direct result of my judicial role in sentencing Bruggs Junior in the Youth Court.

Andy Bruggs himself was hardly a 'person of good character' in judicial parlance. He had a string of previous convictions, all for minor offences of disorderly behaviour and criminal damage.

His Honour Judge Keith Sutler had several trenchant words to say before imposing the inevitable custodial sentence.

To Andy Bruggs' surprise, Judge Keith suspended the

sentence for two years on the strength of our encouraging Restorative Justice dialogue and the report from the RJ coordinator.

During that two-year period Andy was to comply with a probation programme for twenty days of rehabilitation activity to address his thinking skills and anger management, and two hundred hours of unpaid work in the community.

I refrained from attending his case in the public gallery. I had seen more than enough of him and the rest of his motley family.

I was, however, to witness more than one Bruggs case, later in the year.

*

November had arrived, cold and damp – and that was just in the Law Courts building. The flat state-of-the-art roof had sprung a leak, and the rain had found its way through to the ceiling of Magistrates' Court 3. A large yellow plastic bucket now sat on the corner of the prosecutor's desk, and the long, intermittent silences between cases, as the various court officers typed up what they had to type up, were regularly broken by steady drips and splashes like Chinese water torture.

The low early winter temperature had seeped too into the retiring room, as the two large central heating radiators were barely issuing any warmth at all.

There was a reason for this. The Law Courts had been built twelve years previously under a government Private Finance Initiative with a major national construction

company. The deal had obliged the occupier to enter into a twenty-year contract for all maintenance and repair. Only a company employee could carry out any such work (and technically this included the changing of light bulbs and renewing clock batteries).

The employees of the company were based in Bristol, two and a half hours away.

The small print in the maintenance contract explained, furthermore, that the heating system in the court building would be controlled and set by a computer that resided in the company's office basement in Bristol, and which regulated itself according to the weather conditions and ambient temperatures in that fair city.

In consequence, the magistrates and court officers in our own city often resorted to waistcoat or cardigan in summer and shirt sleeve order in winter.

When first opened for business, our spanking new courts had a ferocious air-conditioning system that roared and howled through the courtrooms and corridors like a force 9 severe gale off Cape Horn. Whenever a courtroom door was opened, reams of paper (yes, we had paper in those days) blew like a snowstorm between prosecutor and defence advocate, and were sucked out through the open doorway as though by a monstrous Hoover.

That problem was eventually resolved by disconnecting the air-conditioning altogether.

*

At any rate, here was November – my last month as a sitting magistrate, after twenty-five years in the role.

It was a Youth Court day. Unfortunately the designers of the Law Courts had omitted to cater for the informal layout of a youth courtroom, and so we had to exercise judgement on ten-year-olds from the heights of a Magistrates' Court bench far removed from the small person standing before us in the far distance with his mum or dad.

We three magistrates studied the court list in the (freezing) retiring room at 9:30am.

One entry caught my eye: Bruggs, Daniel. Second listing. Theft from a shop. Not guilty plea entered. Scheduled for trial today. I searched my memory. Daniel. Danny. Wasn't he the younger brother, so promising at school and the apple of his mother's eye? Hey ho. We shall see.

When his case came up, I explained to the court that

I had had dealings with Danny's father as a victim. Would the defence or the prosecution prefer me to 'recuse' myself from presiding at Danny's trial, or were they happy for me to sit on his case?

They were content. And so the trial commenced. Danny sat with his mother Maureen, and his solicitor Mr Whitehead, who was an excellent local defence advocate of many years' standing.

As this was the first time Danny had ever been in a courtroom (Mr Whitehead assured me), I carefully explained to him who the various court officers were and what was to be their role. I emphasised that the important thing was that he should understand what was going on, and if in doubt to raise his hand. Poor lad, he looked genuinely bewildered, but I was encouraged to see that, unlike most young offenders before us, Danny looked me in the eye when responding, and wore an expression of alert intelligence.

The prosecutor duly set out the basic facts of the alleged offence. A group of boys in their school uniforms had entered TK Maxx in the shopping mall at about four o'clock one afternoon. The in-house security officer (I still wanted to call them store detectives) immediately kept an eye on them from a distance, as he recognised one of the boys from a previous attempted shoplifting incident some weeks before.

Four of the boys, he noticed, were clearly close friends and kept together in a close gaggle, fooling around a little as they sauntered through the women's underwear section towards the computer games and smartphones.

The fifth lad, Danny, was clearly on the fringe of the group and trying to join in. After a while he wandered off on his own and mooched around fairly aimlessly, casting long glances across the shop at his school mates in a rather wistful manner.

The security officer was the first witness for the prosecution, and explained that he had noted the boy's movements and manner because he felt rather sorry for him.

However, after fifteen minutes or so the five boys had had enough, and both Danny and his companions wandered back to the entrance together without buying anything. Three of the boys were joshing Danny a bit and pushing him about in a light-hearted manner that nonetheless had a slightly brutal edge, the officer thought.

Danny was not enjoying this, plainly, and was evidently being slightly bullied.

The security officer's attention was then diverted by a call on his walkie-talkie and he went to speak to a colleague at the far end of the shop floor.

At that moment, the entrance-door alarm went off. A customer must have passed through the exit with an item that still had its security tag attached. The officer's colleague immediately ran to the doorway and found Danny standing just outside on the paving, having been abandoned by his school friends, who had all run off rather quickly.

No other customer being in the vicinity, this second officer (on his own evidence as the second prosecution witness) apprehended Danny and asked him to turn out his pockets. This he did without demur, and the officer acknowledged (at cross-examination by Mr Whitehead) that Danny seemed bewildered as to what was happening.

From his left-hand school blazer pocket Danny drew out a slim white box which, on opening, he found to contain a dark blue state-of-the-art Samsung mobile phone.

He was escorted back into the shop to a small office set aside for the purpose, and the police were summoned.

At interview in the police station, Danny denied all knowledge of the phone and rejected every suggestion that he had stolen it.

From there the matter took its inevitable course through the Crown Prosecution Service, leading unavoidably to the trial now before us.

CHAPTER FIFTEEN

This was one of those cases where the defence rested entirely on the defendant's denial, with no witness or substantive evidence available to back up this contention.

The defence advocate therefore has very little material to work with in support of the client. What Mr Whitehead had to do was to try and sow sufficient doubt about Danny's guilt in the minds of the magistrates to make a conviction unsafe.

Danny had a clean record. No previous convictions of any kind. He was doing well at school and was ambitious to go on to further education.

This all helped, but it would never be enough. A trial requires facts.

Mr Whitehead was an old hand at this. He knew that the only effective move would be to undermine the evidence of the prosecution witnesses.

Were either of the security officers' reports really as useful to the prosecution as the CPS had hoped?

Danny had been found standing still outside the shop doors with the stolen phone in his pocket.

Cross-examination of the second officer revealed that the officer had not only thought this odd, but also that Danny had put on a very good show of being genuinely surprised to discover what his pocket contained.

The first officer, under pressure from Mr Whitehead, had admitted that he had kept Danny under surveillance the whole time until he had been called away on his walkie-talkie, and at no time had he seen Danny go anywhere near the mobile phone displays.

The Bench was duly invited by Danny's solicitor to find that the allegation of shoplifting, theft from a shop, had not been proved 'beyond reasonable doubt'.

My colleagues and I promptly retired to consider the verdict, and in a short space of time returned to the courtroom to pronounce Daniel Bruggs 'not guilty'.

His costs would be met by Legal Aid, and we invited his mother to apply for travel expenses to be reimbursed.

The only real issue in our minds as we sat at the retiring-room table had been whether there had existed a realistic opportunity for Danny to walk over to the phone display shelves between the moment the first officer was diverted, and the group of lads re-forming near the checkout before leaving. On the second officer's evidence we thought not.

We therefore concluded that the phone had been 'planted' on Danny, most probably by one of the other boys and very likely as part of the bullying attitude that the first officer had noticed. That, of course, was pure conjecture, but the likelihood provided more than adequate doubt.

There was no denying that Danny had physically taken the item from the shop without paying for it. That, however, is not theft.

There had been no intention 'permanently to deprive' on Danny's part.

*

It is always my practice to talk briefly to the young person at the end of a hearing, whether this is a trial or a sentencing. On this occasion, after the formal verdict pronouncement, I asked Danny to sit down again.

"Now then, Danny," I began, "you are a good lad who has never been in trouble with the police or the court, and you leave this court today with that still being true.

"Your mum can be proud of you. Life is not easy but you have an excellent record at school and, as Mr Whitehead has told us, a keen ambition to get qualifications for a future career.

"It is quite possible – and I put this as no more than a suggestion – that you feel a bit left out from the group of school friends that you wanted to be with on that afternoon in TK Maxx. This experience may well suggest to you that you need to be very careful in choosing the company you keep in future. We would rather agree with you there.

"That will take a bit of courage over the next few years, but we hope you succeed.

"Off you go; and we wish you well. Thank you, Mum, for coming to support Danny today."

I was rewarded with a smile from Mrs Bruggs and a long, thoughtful stare from Daniel before he suddenly stood up and followed his mother from the courtroom.

Well, who knows? Magistrates very rarely get to hear of the positive influence of a court hearing on a defendant. We only become tediously familiar with the unsuccessful results for those who end up appearing regularly before us, sometimes hailing us like old friends.

Would young Daniel manage to shrug off the lifestyle and outlook of his own brother and father, extricate himself from the mire of deprivation and poverty that moulds the Bruggses of this world into hopeless despair, and carve out a life for himself with confidence and serenity?

We shall probably never know.

*

My seventieth birthday was now only days away. His Majesty's Courts & Tribunals Service was digging deep into its pockets to extract the gardening or book token with which it would solemnly express its gratitude for my twenty-five years of free judicial dispensation, before instantly deleting my eJudiciary website account on the stroke of midnight.

I would continue to pay my subscription to the Magistrates Association, whose revenues had been severely hit by the gradual shrinking of the magistracy numbers in recent years.

I would continue to enjoy reading their quarterly magazine, but by remaining a member I would also be able to carry on assisting in schools and adult groups with the Magistrates in the Community programme which I had always enjoyed.

I might also attend an MA annual general meeting if they chose an interesting regional historic city in which to hold it. My wife and I could make a little holiday from it.

CHAPTER SIXTEEN

And so the day of my final court sitting arrived.

The Bench Chairman had done his stuff and circulated all my colleagues with the date of this event. Consequently on entering Courtroom 3 with my two wingers I was met by a sea of familiar faces all smiling at us from the public gallery at the back of the court.

The Bench Chairman stood below the bench and spoke some kind words, and then it was my turn.

To a few raised eyebrows but several nodding heads at the back, I expressed my appreciation particularly to the 'defence community', those local solicitors (two of whom happily were present) who slog away for little recompense in defending those before us, with such dedication and patience; also with much generosity in time and commitment to the courts beyond the strict call of duty.

My words were kindly acknowledged by one of the defence advocates and by the legal adviser. My erstwhile colleagues duly trooped out of the rear door with a farewell wave or two, and we commenced the business of the day.

And guess what. There in the court listing was Bruggs, Wayne; first listing. Breach of post-custodial supervision. Now being eighteen years of age here he was for the first time in the adult court.

He had only been released from Portland YOI three months previously, where he had shouldered his way through every prison regulation and been repeatedly denied early release, to the despair of the staff and the prolonged intimidation of several fellow inmates.

Having returned home to a gruff welcome from his father Andy and deep sighs from his mother, he had chosen to ignore all appointments with his probation officer, and had mooched off to stay several weeks with a mate of his up in Pigdon in the north of the county, without the knowledge or approval of his officer.

Hence his appearance today. We could send him to prison for fourteen days, fine him or take no action. Not much of a choice.

None of these options would remotely succeed in influencing Wayne to obey the rules.

His weary life on the treadmill of anti-social behaviour and surly criminality had now begun to gather pace.

One of my colleagues leaned across to say that she would like us to withdraw to the retiring room to consider an idea she had just had.

We were all agreed that some entirely novel form of motivation was the only hope for Wayne. This might be a keen new interest in some constructive trade or hobby. It might be a new relationship with someone who had the strength of character to take him under their wing and instil a sense of honourable purpose and self-esteem.

Either way, someone somewhere had to be sufficiently within his circle of acquaintance to be prompted or attracted to engage with him.

There was potentially just that person right here in the courthouse. Someone, indeed, dedicated to that role and with an impressive track record with offenders, their families, their victims and their witnesses, both in and out of the Law Courts.

The volunteer Lay Court Chaplain.

Could we not, my colleague suggested, invite him to come into the back of the courtroom to hear us pass sentence on Wayne?

We would impose a fine at a level well beyond Wayne's capability of paying immediately that day, and then in lieu of payment instruct him to remain within the court precincts for the remainder of the morning session.

We would ask the Chaplain to 'keep an eye' on him and have a chat. The Chaplain would understand this coded message, and we would leave the rest up to him. If there was the faintest chance of Wayne finding someone he could trust and open up to, it was worth the gamble.

In any case, we could think of nothing else that would be half as likely to reduce Wayne's future re-offending, and so we returned to the courtroom and pronounced sentence accordingly.

I have often wondered since then whether this little manoeuvre managed to prompt a new direction in the life of that unfortunate young man. I shall never know.

Ordering detention in the court precincts in lieu of a fine is a last resort for the type of penniless down-and-outs of no fixed abode who appear before us in regular shambolic fashion for minor offences such as Drunk and Disorderly in a Public Place. For them it achieves nothing, except somewhere warm and dry to sit for a few hours. The criminal justice system has no answer for such in our society who have reached rock bottom.

This detention provision is probably the last remaining vestige of true traditional summary justice still open for magistrates to use at our discretion. A very long time ago, justices were free to exercise their imagination in imposing appropriate forms of minor punishment, most famously and amusingly illustrated in that splendid novel *The Irish RM* by Somerville and Ross.

O tempora, o mores.

*

At the day's end my colleagues and I shook hands and bid adieu. I looked round the retiring room for the last time, lingering a while after they had gone, recalling my interesting, frustrating, amusing and downright sad experiences there over so many years.

I had engaged with individuals from all walks of life, on the Bench as well as down in front of the bench. Characters and circumstances of life that would otherwise never have crossed my secure middle-class path.

No longer to be addressed as 'your Worship'; no longer to be sworn at from behind the bullet-proof dock glass;

no longer to find myself in the astonishing position of an ordinary representative of the local community sending someone else into prison as part of my routine duties.

No longer to see the spark of understanding in the eye of a youth such as Danny Bruggs as the English criminal justice system achieved one of its rare triumphs.

I turned out the lights and headed for home.

ABOUT THE AUTHOR

Richard Trahair is a retired chartered surveyor, living with his wife Biddy in a tiny rural hamlet, miles from anywhere in particular, where they have resided for almost forty-five years.

During that time he has also been a parish organist for more than thirty years, accompanying services in a number of small churches in the area, with the occasional opportunity to play informally to small handfuls of bemused listeners in a variety of unlikely places such as Wyoming USA, central London, the Isle of Wight, west Cornwall, Rosscarbery Cathedral in Eire, Bamburgh in Northumberland, Poole in Dorset, Framlingham in Suffolk, St Mary's Hunslet Grange, Leeds University church, Lulworth Castle chapel and Harlech in north Wales. He enjoys playing orchestral transcriptions, cannot cope with counterpoint and would really like to have been a Wurlitzer organist in a cinema in the good old days of silent movies.

He has also been a presiding justice in the nearest city Magistrates' Court, where he has served for almost a quarter of a century. There he has (with no legal training of any kind) issued hundreds of thousands of fines, disqualified dozens of drivers, given new hope to many rejected young people and sent a good many rogues to prison. He has also endured hopeless government Court computer programs, sat under dripping courtroom ceilings, and with his long-suffering colleagues has tried to exercise justice, fairness and common sense for both victims of crime and its perpetrators alike.

He has published three adventure novels, and also his reminiscences of managing Church of England property. Of these, three books have been published with The Book Guild.